monsoonbooks

THE DEATH OF SALLY SONG

Following stints as a caregiver, stage actor and researcher, Singapore-based Julianne Cheah settled on a technical role in a large organisation but never lost her dream of writing a novel. *The Death of Sally Song* is her first novel.

The Death of Sally Song

Julianne Cheah

monsoon

monsoonbooks

First published in 2022
by Monsoon Books Ltd
www.monsoonbooks.co.uk

No.1 The Lodge, Burrough Court,
Burrough on the Hill, Melton Mowbray LE14 2QS, UK

ISBN (paperback): 9781915310026
ISBN (ebook): 9781915310033

Cover design by Cover Kitchen.

A Cataloguing-in-Publication data record is available from the British
Library.

For my parents, with love

This is home, truly

'Home' by Dick Lee (1998)

Dramatis Personae

In alphabetical order

Ah Pa   Mr Tang Choon Wee, a taxi driver. Father of Mei.

Alex Toh   An accountant. About to marry Tang Siew Ling.

Auntie Fong   Mrs Chan, nee Lai Siew Fong, she is the sole proprietor of the Can-Do bookshop and Mei's boss. Mother of Inspector Chan Teck Wai.

Auntie Geok   Madam Neo Geok Lin is the sole proprietor of June's Fashion.

Auntie Kim   Madam Loh Bee Kim. Mother to Alex Toh. Housewife.

Auntie Ratna   Mrs Ratna Agrawal. Together with her husband, the proprietors of Jaipur Carpets. Mother to Lakshmi.

Auntie Rosnah   Madam Rosnah binte Salleh is the sole proprietor of Qurayes Fashion. Mother to Nik.

Beng   Tang Beng Siew, an electrical engineer. Mei's eldest brother.

Chan Teck Wai   An inspector based in the Police Cantonment Complex. Auntie Fong's son.

Chloe Teng	A Secondary 4 student at Alexandra Secondary School.
Cora Lim	An accountant. Married to Tang Beng Siew.
Jeevan Kanagasabhai	A teacher at Alexandra Secondary School.
John Kong	A teacher at Alexandra Secondary School.
Lakshmi	Daughter of Mr and Mrs Agrawal, she is a Secondary 4 student at Alexandra Secondary School.
Ling	Tang Siew Ling, Mei's sister. An accountant.
Ma	Madame Yoon Bee Lay, a housewife. Mother of Mei.
Maggie	Maggie Lee. Mei's friend. Studying Chemical and Biological Engineering in Nanyang Technological University.
Mary Wong	The mother of Sally Song.
Matt	Mr Matthew Li is the sole proprietor of Music Matt.
Mei	Tang Siew Mei. A fresh graduate working as a secondhand bookshop assistant.
Muhammad Rizwan	A station inspector based in the Police Cantonment Complex.
Nik	Nik bin Abdullah. Son of Madam Rosnah, he is a Secondary 4 student at Alexandra Secondary School.
Nora	Nora Yusuf. Mei's friend. A public relations officer.

Richard Lim	Richard Lim is the sole proprietor of Robert's Photos.
Richard Toh	Father to Alex Toh. Retired.
Seetoh Yi Wei	A teacher at Alexandra Secondary School.
Shanti	Shanti Kulkarni. A law graduate doing her pupillage. Mei's best friend since Primary 1.
Sharmini	Sharmini Pillai. Mei's friend. A teacher at Alexandra Secondary School. Teaches Mathematics and Physics.
Song Wei Lin, Sally	A Secondary 4 student at Alexandra Secondary School.
Song Wing Hock, Jimmy	The father of Sally Song.
Tan Yock Li	A Secondary 4 student at Alexandra Secondary School.
Uncle Nathan	Mr Nathan Agrawal. Together with his wife, the proprietors of Jaipur Carpets. Father to Lakshmi.
Uncle Seng	Mr Wang Lee Seng is the sole proprietor of Astara KTV Karaoke Lounge.
Wong Yi Ling	A teacher at Alexandra Secondary School. Teaches Art and Design.
Yong	Yong Sim Yan. Mei's friend. A National University of Singapore student in the second tier of the Architecture course.

22 Feb | Saturday

We met for dinner first. Of course, we would need to fuel up before we danced the night away. I thought we'd be eating nearer to the club but Shanti decreed that we would eat further away as the places nearby would be packed with other clubgoers.

We ended up meeting at McDonald's.

'Ooh … so cute,' cooed Nora as she took in Maggie's sparkly top and flirty skirt. 'Exactly right for dancing! And the shoes are the best.'

'Aren't they?' Maggie peered down at her sequinned sneakers. 'Matt said they'd be the most comfortable for dancing.'

Fair and dainty, Maggie's outfit made her look like a teenage fairy. Her parents are really strict and she's not very comfortable with revealing outfits so Matt had kept it modest but fun.

'Who's having what?' asked Shanti. 'I'm going to buy.'

Nora and Maggie held the table while Shanti and I joined the queue for burgers.

'I think I'm having a Big Mac set and a shake,' I pondered, studying the menu.

'It's disgusting the way you eat,' Shanti griped. 'Given how small you are, you just eat and eat and stay the same size while I only have to look at fries to gain weight!'

'It's all that sitting around you lawyers do. I, on the other hand, am constantly on my — Watch the hair!' I cried as Shanti aimed a swipe at my head. 'Not that you could shift it — Matt put so much gel.'

'Matt dressed you?' Shanti queried.

'What do you think? Maggie is clueless and I am useless when it comes to this kind of thing. We had to bribe him to help us out — two eclairs, chocolate and coffee.'

I looked down at my black PVC dress, boots and clutch.

'Not bad, huh? Considering we got all of it in Holland Village, including make-up. Lucky we went shopping last week. We couldn't find anything in my size. Had to get this taken in. Auntie Win was laughing like crazy.'

'I was wondering about the make-up. I've never seen you in more than lip gloss — Yes, we'll have two Big Macs, one cheeseburger and one McChicken, all sets with Coke — no three Cokes and one Sprite.'

'And I'll have a strawberry milkshake. Yup, Auntie Win let us get dressed in her changing room then Matt did our make-up.'

It took two trays to carry all the food back to the table.

'It was so much fun!' Maggie was saying. 'Matt is really good at picking out clothes. I was a bit worried at first — there were so many choices and I didn't have a clue. Mei just looked around and said "The hell with it! I'm going to get expert help." Then she went off and came back with Matt.'

'It went a lot faster after that.'

'More like "It went a lot faster after you gave in about The Bag."'

'The Bag? Oh ya, I don't see it,' said Nora.

Maggie laughed. 'Matt insisted that he wasn't going to waste his time dressing us if she was going to spoil it all by carrying The Bag.'

'Nothing wrong with The Bag!' I grumped. 'It's the only one big enough to carry everything I need.' I missed The Bag, as everybody calls it, usually making a face. It is a satchel that I picked up at the army supplies shop when I started uni. Actually, I'd wanted the one in camouflage but since, as Shanti pointed out, I spent very little time in the jungle, I'd gotten the olive green one instead.

It goes everywhere with me and carries everything I need. Made of hard-wearing, waterproof canvas, it holds a lot! Umbrella (the Singaporean American Express: Don't leave home without it! Rain or shine you'll need it), bus guide, water bottle (I get thirsty), first aid kit, sewing kit, notebook, sweater (sometimes the aircon gets too cold, especially when you come inside from the hot outside), snacks — you name it, I had it in The Bag. These days, I don't carry many library books but I still like having a book with me to read on the bus and I keep a hard folder in there in case I have to keep any paper uncrumpled.

'Wah!!! So, what do you have in that teeny tiny thing?' Nora snatched my clutch and upended it on the table.

'Oi! You're going to get tomato sauce on my stuff!'

'Keys, packet tissue, NRIC and Transitlink … oh and $40 in the pocket. That's not going to buy you many drinks.'

'Wow, you must be feeling so naked … you don't even have your pager.'

'Wait, no phone card? Ya, I am feeling sooo naked and extremely insecure so don't make me cry — as it is the false eyelashes are making my eyes itch.' I lifted a finger to scratch the annoying weight on my eyelids.

'Don't rub!' cried Maggie and smacked my hand down.

After eating, we took a cab to Zouk. Shanti got the front seat and the rest of us fit in the back.

Wow! The queue or rather the crowd outside the club was huge. Well, it was Saturday night after all.

Most of them looked like university students. There were also the sarong party girls in tight tube tops and super-short skirts, clinging to the arms of their ang moh boyfriends, mostly overweight with thinning hair, all sweating like crazy in the humid night. Although, I'm not sure if you should call them 'boyfriends' because some of them looked like they were nearer sixty than sixteen.

An hour later, we got our hands stamped and finally made it into the club. To my disgust but not surprise, the bouncers stopped only me, so the others went on ahead while I had to stay back and dig out my NRIC to show them.

Just entering the club itself was an experience. Going through the smoky tunnel, I followed the others at a distance, distracted by everything that was going on. You could hear the thumping of music, people talking, laughing, a dizzying kaleidoscope of sight and sound.

Although Maggie and I were DBM ('Dressed by Matt'), Nora and Shanti didn't need his help to look good. Nora, slim and fine-boned, looks elegant regardless of what she wears. Tonight, she was wearing a black slip dress over a white t-shirt with white sneakers. Her pixie cut, just like Demi Moore's, was slicked down.

If I could only use one word to describe Shanti, it would be 'statuesque'. Hard to believe that once upon a time I was taller than she was. Unfortunately, while I stopped growing at about 10, she just kept on and on; I think she grew her last cm in her second year of university. She doesn't dress up outside work unless she has to (i.e. her parents will be present) so she was just wearing faded hip-hugging jeans and a cropped red t-shirt that showed off her curves. Her only make-up was a red lipstick. Her long glossy black hair was casually twisted and tucked under. Even so, I watched men's heads turn as she went by. You really don't need to dress up when you look that good dressed down. I sighed with envy.

In the club, the dancefloor was packed. Barely room to move but still people were managing to dance like the world was going to end tomorrow.

With the strobe lights and the other fancy laser stuff, I was worried that I wouldn't be able to find the girls. But from a few steps above the dancefloor, I spotted Shanti and eeled my way to them, wishing I had thought of ear plugs.

Techno's really not my thing. Normally, I like stuff I can hum along to; in other words, music that actually has a tune. But in a club, you're surrounded by the sound and it becomes another experience altogether. Monotonous and repetitious becomes tribal and hypnotic. You lose track of time and the thumping bass takes over the beating of your heart. You become a part of it, oblivious to everything except the pulsing rhythm ... and your bladder.

Forty minutes later I really needed to pee. I tapped Shanti on the shoulder and pointed to the toilets. She nodded but gestured

'Drinks?' I nodded then signed 'Where?' She looked around and waved towards the seating area. I nodded but as I turned to go, I felt a hand catch my arm. Maggie wanted to go too.

The queue for the toilets was long and I was pretty desperate by the time I got into a stall. Wah! The relief! No more toilet paper so I just used a tissue — shh … don't tell anyone. People keep telling me that it clogs up the pipes but seriously, if there's no toilet paper, what do you expect me to do? Walk around smelling of pee?

Someone was throwing up in the next stall. Sounded pretty bad, like she was already empty but unable to stop. Finally the retching ended, just as I was pulling down my skirt.

We emerged at the same time, my toilet neighbour and I. She was swaying slightly, pale as a ghost, her eyes were red and her mascara was running. Her bobbed hair was limp, like she had used up even the energy from there. Even so, she still looked vaguely familiar … like I knew her from somewhere?

'Are you okay?' I asked as I held the door for her.

She nodded but if anything, she got even paler when she looked at me. I pushed my way through the chattering crowd to the fountain sink, a colourful tiled creation that was trying to be artistic and turned to let the poor thing have first go but she was gone. Eww … she definitely hadn't washed her hands or washed out her mouth.

'Mei! Thanks for waiting!' Maggie had joined me.

'No prob. Let's go get our drinks.' I was ready for a drink. Even with the aircon, the exercise and the sheer body heat emanated by the other dancers had heated the space until I could feel the sweat running down my back.

Shanti had managed to get a table. Somewhat near the entrance but I wasn't complaining. We were all pretty much ready for a rest. Talk about no stamina.

We sat around chilling. People milled about, coming, going, meeting, parting.

Not much conversation as the music was way too loud. As I watched them set up the stage for the live performance, a familiar face passed us on the way out. Toilet Girl was leaving.

The next few hours passed in a blur of pulsing music and gyrating bodies. We stumbled out drunk on the beat, just in time to take the last bus home. After all, I had to work tomorrow.

23 Feb | Sunday, Jiak Kim Street

On the Singapore River, a boat floated as the men onboard captured floating rubbish with a big net. A bumboat chugged downriver to find its place among the others waiting for the tourists to find them.

On land, the little road sweeper was peacefully sweeping up the detritus from the night before, thriftily crushing then stowing the empty beer and drinks cans in the plastic bag tied at his waist. Empty plastic packets fluttered about, blown by the wind into the alley between the club and the construction site fence. He followed them into the alley.

As he swept up the litter, his eye was caught by movement further in. He walked over to get a closer look. A young girl lay sprawled, skirt aflutter in the wind, face turned away as if asleep but ants were busily crawling around and over her fearlessly, as though she was a fallen tree in the jungle.

Finally, he got close enough to smell her.

* * *

The police inspector squatted by the girl and pondered. He'd taken all the photos he needed and was waiting for the crime scene specialists to show up.

He stared at her face. So young and still somebody had killed her.

Without any sign of an NRIC, it was going to be damn difficult to find out who she was. Even with the crowds of people who were here last night, it was unlikely that anybody would come forward.

But what was seriously puzzling him was the scattered Panda candy that surrounded her like a sunny halo.

25 Feb | Tuesday

When I woke up on Tuesday morning, I could feel my t-shirt sticking to my skin with sweat. I really felt icky. Even my bedsheet was damp with sweat! The fan was still going, valiantly circulating the hot, humid air which did not reach me. Ling must have adjusted its direction in the night, the bitch.

Ah Pa doesn't believe in air conditioning at least not for his children. In the flat, there is only one room with air-conditioning — the master bedroom. Not that Ma appreciates it. Every night there's a fight over the temperature — she hates being cold and will tell you in great detail how aircon causes fong sup, what torture she suffers every morning and how Ah Pa is a brute for making her sleep in aircon.

But even so, I wish we had aircon in the bedroom or at least a second fan that could be directly blowing on me; another cause of fong sup but who cares? Maybe I should buy another fan. It's just too hot, too humid … even in shorts and a tank top, sweat gathers in every crevice.

My Malaysian friends tell me it's a real shock to the system when they first come to Singapore. Amazing, given that we're just south of them. One of them, Jasmine, claims that she spent her first week here flat on her back because of the humidity. It just saps everything out of you. I guess it's like walking around in a steam bath. The moisture makes the air thick and heavy, so you feel like you're weighed down.

I didn't have the energy to shift myself. I felt flaccid, no backbone ... no muscles. I couldn't move, couldn't think ...

Oh ... why do I never remember that I should not start reading murder mysteries at night? It's a 'once you start, cannot stop' kind of thing. For me, anyway.

I somehow gathered up the energy to slither down from my upper bunk bed. Oh no ... Ling's bed was already made. That meant she had already left for work. What time was it? I picked up my watch — die, it was already eight-thirty — I was going to be late for work!

Suddenly, I was moving. First to the washbasin to brush teeth then dive into the shower for a wet down and wipe dry. Run back to bedroom and pull on clothes. Okay, didn't quite wipe dry but good enough.

All in all, I managed to get ready and out of the house in twenty minutes flat. Breakfast was just going to have to wait. Ma yelled after me 'Lock the gate!' I sighed and made a U-turn to lock the gate before I dashed down the stairs, taking them two at a time.

On a normal day it takes something like an hour, hour and a half to get from the West Coast to Holland Village, given the time taken waiting for buses to show up. Today, all the connections happened with barely any waiting time. Luck takes pity on fools. I made it to the shop in record time, but still ten minutes late.

'Sorry! Sorry!' I panted as I ran up to Auntie Fong, who was stooping down to pull up the roller door.

'Aiyah! Why so late ha?' she scolded. 'My back so pain, I

had to bend down, open the door, everything!'

'Yes, yes, I know! So sorry! Overslept.' I took over pulling out the posts while she stood back and folded her arms.

'Wah! What were you doing last night till you cannot wake up? Pak tor, is it?' Auntie Fong is always much more amiable once she got things off her chest.

This feisty lady started the bookshop to support herself and her son after her husband passed away. He was a police officer who was killed while trying to break up a fight. Apparently one of the assailants had a knife and stuck it in his belly. I heard it took him a week to die from the blood poisoning.

Initially, Can-Do was only half a shop, which she shared with Auntie Win who does alterations, then it grew to become the Can-Do bookshop that I know and love. She's around Ma's age, so fifty plus?

'No lah! I was reading that Sara Paretsky mystery last night – so exciting I couldn't stop. Three o'clock, I was still awake. Her books dam' shiok one.'

Auntie Fong shook her head at me. 'Aiyah, get married lah! All this read, read, read, hor, spoil your eyes only! At least if got husband, got something to do at night!'

'Ooh ... do what aaa...?' I asked, knowing very well what she was talking about. We've had this conversation more than once.

'You know laa ...'

'Donno leh ...'

'You aaa ... I know you know lah!' She poked me in the shoulder lightly with her finger, laughing.

Auntie Fong is somewhat concerned that I'm not married,

without even a boyfriend. Keeps telling me that I'm wasting my life, I should look for a husband, I should get married. And that I'm going to regret it when I'm old if I don't have children to look after me.

'What to do? No one wants to marry me!' I sighed somewhat melodramatically.

'Wear a dress, put on some make-up … Sure got man wan' one!' She winked an eye and gave me the thumbs-up.

'Huh! And if I'm in a dress, who's going to carry the books and climb the ladder?'

'If you get married, I can hire a nice strong boy. Good-looking one with big muscles!' she leered.

'Wah! If Teck Wai hears you …'

'Hmph! He's another one. Work, work, work only! How to find a wife?'

'I'm sure there are a lot of nice young policewomen where he works.'

'I keep telling him he should ask you to go out.'

'Cannot lah! Every time we meet we fight like cats and dogs.'

'Hai yah! This kind of fighting is good for being married. You fight and fight but still friendly what!'

Huh? Fighting is good for a relationship? That's something I had to think about. Ah Pa and Ma rarely fight except about the aircon temperature. Mainly because he's usually out driving his taxi. One might think that the reason they don't fight is that they don't spend many waking hours together.

By the time we'd set up the shelves outside, stuck newspapers in the racks, pushed out the boxes of clearance books and opened up the cash register, Auntie Fong was ready for her morning break.

I wandered through the shop with a feather duster, dusting off the tops and backs of the books. On tiptoe I could just about reach the top shelves with the tip of the feather duster. With the number of bookshelves, that took some time.

Looking up, I noticed the beginnings of cobwebs in a corner of the ceiling and cursed silently. I was going to need to get the long stick to clean it out, failing which I would have to go down and borrow the ladder. The step stool I used to reach the higher shelves was not going to be high enough to reach that corner. No help for it, it was going to have to wait.

Never mind, I got the broom and swept the floor. Didn't take too long with most of the floor space covered with bookshelves but the smooth linoleum seemed to have some sticky stuff here and there, so I had to get the mop out too. With a bit of water and a touch of hard rubbing, the sticky stuff came off — what was it? Someone must have spilled a drink.

There didn't seem to be many people around, so I picked up Auntie Fong's *Straits Times* and laid it out over the children's books display.

Headline: 'Security tightened ahead of Deng's funeral'. As expected.

One hundred and seventy-seven dead in a fire in Baripada? Where was Baripada? I laid down the paper and went over to the shelf for extra-large books. There was a huge atlas there somewhere if nobody had bought it yet. Ah, there it was. In Orissa, 2011 km southeast of Delhi.

I turned the page over and there a sketch of Toilet Girl looked up at me. Found dead off Jiak Kim Street on Sunday morning. Police seeking information. I felt a chill wash over me. She was dead. She must have died mere hours after I saw her. How did she die? It can't have been natural causes — she was so young. Did she kill herself? Could I have done something to prevent it? That's ridiculous! I didn't even know who she was … did I?

She looked so familiar but I just couldn't put my finger on it. Given her fearful reaction when she saw me, it seems like she knew me though.

'What are you looking at?' Auntie Fong, back from her morning break, looked down then came around to look over my shoulder.

'This girl. The police are trying to find out who she is.' I showed her the sketch. I thought it was a pretty good sketch, even though it was completely expressionless.

She considered it for a while, wrinkling her nose as she concentrated.

'Isn't she that girl from Alexandra Secondary School?'

'Huh?'

'You know lah, that girl! Always comes in to buy special offer M&Bs.'

'Oh ya!' I picked up the phone and, checking the number provided, tried to call the police. Engaged.

Ten minutes later … engaged.

Half an hour later … engaged. I put down the receiver and slumped. Auntie Fong patted me consolingly.

'Aiyaaa … always like that one! You have to go down to Cantonment Complex.'

'Ummmph …' That didn't sound like fun. It was, I knew,

really hot outside, while it was nice and cool inside with the aircon.

She continued brightly. 'You can go after the lunch crowd. I'll buy back and then you can go. But must come back by 4 pm, ya?'

I finally left the shop at about 2 pm, by which time I was so hungry that I had to buy a luncheon meat bun to eat on the way to the bus stop. Even so, by the time I reached Chinatown, I couldn't take it anymore and ducked into a nearby coffee shop for a quick meal.

I finally got to the Police Cantonment Complex at about 3 pm. At the glass-walled counter, I handed over my NRIC to the young police officer to take down my details, stated my business and was sent to sit in the waiting area.

About ten minutes later, a stern-looking officer came up to me. 'Madam Tang? I'm Station Inspector Muhammad Rizwan. Please follow me.'

As I followed him, I studied his back. His hair was cut very short, probably regulation, and over his white shirt he wore a jacket. Wise, because the place was cold. In the ten minutes I'd been waiting, the sweat I'd worked up walking over from the coffee shop in the sun seemed to have frozen on my skin and was sucking up every bit of heat in my body. Even with my sweater on.

He brought me to a small glass-walled room, just big enough for a small table and three chairs, and invited me to sit.

'So, Madam Tang, what can you tell me?'

No beating around the bush for Station Inspector Muhammad Rizwan.

'Err … it's just Miss, I mean Ms. Actually, just call me Mei. I can't tell you much. It's just that you were asking for information about the girl found on Jiak Kim Street. So I, I mean we, that is Auntie Fong, I mean, Mrs Chan …'

He held up his hand. 'Relax, Miss Tang. Take a breath and start from the beginning.'

This was embarrassing. I closed my eyes and calmed myself. Start again.

'Well, it actually started on Saturday night when I saw her in the toilet at Zouk. I thought she looked familiar then, so when I saw the sketch of her in the newspaper, it caught my attention. My boss, Mrs Chan, to whom I showed the sketch, says that she's from Alexandra Secondary School … that's all …' I trailed off. Come all the way here just for that. I waited for him to tell me not to waste his time.

But he smiled.

'Miss Tang, first of all, thank you for coming all the way here to tell me this. Actually, Alexandra Secondary School has already contacted us and given us the girl's details. However, I'm more interested in what you can tell me about Saturday night.'

He went over my entire account, getting every detail on my contact with Toilet Girl for the next thirty minutes. What was she wearing? Was she carrying anything? What time did I see her leave? I am not good with such details and I ummed and ahhed a lot. When he was finally satisfied, he thanked me again and opened the door for me.

'So … what was her name?'

'I'm afraid I can't tell you at this time.'

'How did she die? Did she kill herself?' I was surprised by

how emotional I sounded. 'Was there something I should have done?' I almost wailed.

He seemed taken aback for a moment and then his face softened.

'No, I'm very sure there was nothing you could have done to help her. She was murdered.'

My jaw dropped in shock.

'Sir!'

I turned to see who was calling and, to our mutual surprise, Teck Wai and I came eye to eye. Actually it was eye to chest because he's quite a bit taller than I am. I had to look up to meet his eyes.

He was also wearing a white shirt with the sleeves rolled up. Was this the standard office wear for inspectors? He had an identification tag on a blue and white lanyard around his neck. In the picture on the ID, he was in uniform.

'Mei? What are you doing here? Is my mother okay? Why are you with Inspector Rizwan?'

'Inspector Chan, I hope that when you interview witnesses, you actually give them time to answer.' Inspector Rizwan said sternly.

Teck Wai subsided. I sniggered and he shot me a dirty look.

'Relax, your mum is fine. Oh no! I promised her I'd be back by 4 pm. Got to run!'

'Wait a minute, Miss Tang. Is there a number I can reach you at?'

'Page me.' I rattled off my number and dashed out the door.

* * *

Police Cantonment Complex

Inspector Rizwan counted the digits that Mei had recited, 'Can't be right. One number missing.'

'Typical,' said Teck Wai and rolled his eyes. 'My mother should have her pager number. I'll ask her …'

'She works for your mother?'

'Ya. When she was studying, she started to come to my mom's shop to rent books. Then when I joined up, she started helping my mom out and next thing I knew she was working at the shop. I guess she's okay lah.' he ended on a disgruntled tone.

'Why so not happy? You don't like her, is it?'

Teck Wai shuddered.

'Since Mei is the right age, single and gets along with her, my mother keeps suggesting that I should ask her out. Never mind I'm not interested, never mind I'm too busy, all the time it's "Ah Wai ah, Mei this", "Ah Wai ah, Mei that' … wah piang! Headache only!"

'Ah … I remember that. My mak was exactly the same. But, you know, if you are planning to get married maybe —'

'Aiyo! Tolong ah!' Teck Wai clutched at his hair. 'Don' start can or not?'

26 Feb | Wednesday

Auntie Rosnah came by while I was dusting the books. As usual, she was dressed to impress, today in flowing navy pants with an embroidered, dark grey tunic and, to top it all, a fantastic turban in a dusty violet.

Unfortunately, as the storm colours indicated, she wasn't in a good mood. Her generous, normally smiling, mouth drooped disconsolately and her eyes, even with false eyelashes, looked tired.

'Mei ah, you went to university, right?'

'Ya ...?'

'What do you need to get into university?'

'Hmmm ... well it really depends on what you want to do. Courses like Science or Engineering have very different requirements than Literature. Some more, got quota so ...'

She frowned. 'I don't even know what that boy wants to do. When I try to talk to him about it, he just laughs and runs away. Some more, O-levels coming and he still main-main!'

'Why don't you get Mei to talk to him?' asked Auntie Fong from behind her newspaper. 'He and Lakshmi always come and chichi chacha with her.'

I started to deny it but Auntie Rosnah turned back to me eagerly. 'Can ah, Mei?'

I sighed. How does one get a teenage boy to sit and talk? I still remembered my brother, Beng, at fifteen, communicating in grunts and shrugs. My parents had been at their wits' end. Even though Nik was more talkative than Beng, trying to get him to talk about such things would be difficult. Hmmm …

'It's going to take some money to buy Swensen's for him, Lakshmi and me, okay?'

'Why Lakshmi?' asked Auntie Fong.

'How do you think I'm going to get him to talk to me? I'm going to lure him with food. And if it's three of us, then he won't feel like I'm trapping him so it'll be easier to talk.'

Auntie Rosnah sighed. 'Okay.'

'No guarantee ah!'

* * *

'Hello?'

'Mei! I want to eat ABC!'

* * *

'So, what you been busy with?' Shanti asked as she carefully brought down the height of her ice kacang. The neon bright red, green and yellow syrups that soaked into the shaved ice had melded and darkened into slush before, satisfied, she scooped up a spoonful.

I stirred my chendol to mix the drizzle of gula melaka into the creamy coconut milk.

'Same old same — Oh! I went to Cantonment Complex

yesterday.'

'What for?'

'Did you see that sketch of a girl in the *Straits Times*? Wait a minute.' I dug in The Bag and pulled out the folder with the article I'd clipped from Auntie Fong's copy of *ST* when she was done with it.

Handing her the article, I continued, 'Turns out she was regular at the shop. I couldn't get through on the phone so Auntie Fong said I should go down to Cantonment.'

'All the way there just to tell them that?' Shanti studied the picture.

I shrugged but I already felt the prickling of tears again. Why is it that this keeps happening whenever I think of Toilet Girl? I didn't even know her that well. I blinked hard.

'Turns out, they already knew who she was but the inspector asked me a lot of questions about when I saw her last Saturday night.'

'When did you see her?' Shanti gasped.

I sighed. 'First time in the toilet when I went with Maggie, then when we were sitting down, I saw her leaving. I even spoke to her in the toilet, but I didn't recognize her.'

Shanti digested that for a while. 'But why were they asking you so many questions?'

I gulped. 'She was murdered.'

'What???'

I hushed her but heads turned — her voice really carries. Nothing to see here, folks.

Shanti lowered her voice but continued. 'How do you know she was murdered?'

'I asked the inspector.'

She gave me a disbelieving look. 'And he told you? Just like that?'

'Well, I was upset ... I thought she killed herself.'

'So do the police think you're involved?'

'No lah! He was just trying to confirm the timeline ... or something. He didn't tell me anything.'

'What do you mean "confirm the timeline"? This isn't the US, you know. You read too many murder mysteries.'

'There's no way I could have killed her. I was with you guys until we all went home together.' I grinned at her, 'See, I even have witnesses to my whereabouts.'

'You aaa!' Shanti grumbled. 'I hope you aren't planning to kaypoh in a police investigation.'

'Who? Me?' I blinked innocently.

27 Feb | Thursday

'Ah Fong ah, Mei can come and jaga my shop, eh sai boh? Very urgent!' Auntie Geok called over.

Auntie Fong nodded and waved me over to the shop selling fashion accessories. Auntie Geok sold all kinds of pretty bits and pieces, from earrings, necklaces, hair clips and scrunchies to pantyhose, stockings and socks.

While I was rearranging the hair accessories, Lakshmi came in with a couple of other girls also wearing the Alexandra Secondary School uniform.

She waved to me and headed over to the stockings.

The other two went to the hairclip section and started going through the selection. Or rather one of them was while the other one was just watching her.

'Are you looking for anything specific?' I asked the seeker after a while. With her hair cut into a sleek bob à la Zoe Tay, I could see why she was looking for a hairclip; whenever she looked down, her hair fell like a curtain over her face; must be very troublesome when you are eating.

'Oh, no …' she looked up briefly and her hair fell back. She was very fair, with small, sweet features in a heart-shaped face but I could see her eyes were reddened and a little swollen.

'Are you —'

'Hi, Mei!' Lakshmi called to me. 'Do you have these stockings in XS?'

'Sure …' I looked at the red-eyed girl again but she seemed to have forgotten all about me and was back at the hairclips.

I went over and pulled out a couple of XS stockings in black from the stock drawer and handed them to Lakshmi.

'Why do you want XS stockings, anyway? There's no way they'll fit you — Ow!' She had pinched me quite hard.

'Shh … I just wanted to get you away from Yock Li,' she whispered.

'Why?' I asked, rubbing my arm.

'We just found out that our schoolmate was killed,' she whispered back.

'How did you find out?' I was a little too loud and she pinched me again. I looked over my shoulder guiltily.

The third girl sidled over to join us and said in an undertone 'They called a special assembly to tell us that Sally was found dead. We're not supposed to talk about it.'

'Was that her name? Sally?'

'Ya, Sally Song.'

I looked over my shoulder at Yock Li, still picking through the hairclips like her life depended on it. 'Were they close?'

'No!' snapped Third Girl. Her vehemence sent my eyebrows up. Why was she so angry? It was a completely reasonable question. Was she the Third Girl in reality? Not Agatha Christie's for sure.

'Donno?' Lakshmi shrugged. 'But Yock Li was so upset when she heard that I guess she must've been.'

'How do you know Sally was killed?'

Lakshmi shot me this 'you think I'm stupid or what' look.

'Because they told us that the police might be wanting to talk to some of us.' That makes sense ... I suppose. I didn't think that they would announce it to the whole school.

'Oh ...' I said. 'That's so sad. Did you know Sally well?'

'She was so troublesome,' sniffed Third Girl. 'Always bothering Yock Li. "Yock Li, this", "Yock Li, that" all the time!'

Lakshmi looked at her in surprise.

'She was okay what ... I didn't know her that well. Not in my class,' she explained in an aside to me. 'But she seemed nice and helpful. I even saw her helping to clean the canteen before ...'

'She was getting paid for that.' Third Girl was very definite. 'She got meals in exchange for that.'

'Really? How did you know that?'

'Yock Li asked her about it once; why was she cleaning the canteen and she just said it like this: "They're giving me lunch". No shame one.'

'Wow ... was she so short of money?'

But Lakshmi was starting to get angry.

'Why should she be ashamed? If you don't have money to buy food, why should you be ashamed of working to get food? What? You think it's shameful to be poor, is it?'

'Shh ... she's coming over,' I hissed.

'I want this one,' Yock Li said, holding out a pair of pretty pink hair clips.

'Sure,' I took the packet and headed to the cash register, detouring to check the price. I reached the cash register at the same time as Auntie Geok. She shooed me off and took over, so

I wandered back to Lakshmi.

'Mei, have you seen Nik? Or rather has Auntie Rosnah seen Nik?' Lakshmi asked before I could ask her more about Sally.

'No, why?'

She grimaced, 'He showed me his teacher's note.'

'Ooh! That doesn't sound good.'

'It's not. He's been getting duck eggs in some of the pop quizzes. Consistently!' she rolled her eyes. 'He was laughing when he showed me the note. Seriously! Doesn't he realise the O-levels are just four months away?'

'Aiyo! So how?'

'Donno lah! Auntie Rosnah is going to kill him.'

* * *

Beng Siew and his wife, Cora, came for dinner that night. Yes, he of the grunt and shrug. Thank goodness, he's much improved. Even managed to persuade a woman to marry him. I must say that I hadn't expected that. Of course, he looks much better now that the acne has subsided and the scarring isn't too bad. And he has a job! An electronics engineer, the first university graduate in the family, he is Ma's pride and joy. And once he and Cora have kids …

Ma always cooks a lot whenever he comes over. He and Cora finally moved out end of last year and she misses him. What to do? Only son.

Tonight, our not very big dinner table was covered with so many dishes we had barely any room to put our rice plates or bowls. There was beef with kai lan, tau yew bak with eggs and taukwa, steamed prawns and a stir-fried mix of cauliflower and broccoli. Oh, and salted vegetable and tofu soup. There's always a soup at dinner except when we're having porridge. Ah Gong used to joke that Ma is really Cantonese and was switched at birth.

'Wah!' Beng Siew enthused as he sat down. 'All my favourites! Jiak, everybody!'

Ma beamed but Ah Pa, who doesn't like leftovers, complained, 'Too much food! We eat all, get fat. Don't finish, wasted!' But he picked up his bowl of rice, which I had just put down in front of him, and his chopsticks.

'No problem!' Beng Siew laughed as he started to help himself to the beef. 'We can pack all the leftovers back!'

Cora smiled tightly. 'Maybe I should come for cooking lessons with Ma.'

I shuddered as I squeezed in beside her. 'No. Really. She is the worst cooking teacher.'

'How can you say that?' Ma was indignant.

'You forgot, is it? That time you were teaching me to stir-fry vegetables? Ten minutes only then you took the knife and told me to go away!'

'Hmph, you were too slow.'

I looked at Cora. 'See?' She laughed and her eyes twinkled.

She was my sister, Ling's, classmate in Ngee Ann Poly but while Ling joined an audit firm, Cora decided she'd rather work in a small company and joined the finance department of a local SME, where she does everything from bookkeeping to taxes to payroll. She doesn't make as much money as Ling but gets home at a reasonable hour most days. Priorities, priorities, priorities.

Beng met her when she and Ling were working on a project for class and it was love at first sight. For him anyway. She took a bit of persuading.

'Eh, Mei! Have you heard from NIE yet?' Ah Pa had decided it was time to change the subject.

Oh no. When I graduated, he made me put in an application to the National Institute of Education to train as a teacher. I'd jumped through all the hoops that they required of applicants too but even so …

'She has,' Ma said. 'Last Friday. Did you accept already?'

'Umm … I haven't decided yet.'

'Aiyah! What do you think you're going to do with a degree in Literature? Can only teach.'

'I'm actually thinking of studying journalism.'

'What? You want to study some more?' Ah Pa was appalled. 'Where got money?'

'Even if I go to NIE, I'm going to be studying some more!'

'At least you go to NIE, we know you got job!'

And so the argument wound to its foregone conclusion and I agreed that I would send in my acceptance in the morning.

Auntie Rosnah's problem is really that there's only her and Nik. If she had as many people as we had at the dinner table, he wouldn't have been able to escape.

28 Feb | Friday

Old Mrs Koh was returning a stack of romances. She likes romances, the steamier the better. But her key criteria is that the books be short.

'I'm so old already, I don't want to wait so long before I reach the juicy part!' she said. She means the sex.

'You could just skip to that part?'

'Cheh! Pay so much money, I die die must read every single word! Otherwise wasted!'

This being the case, she reads mainly M&Bs and Silhouette romances. Barbara Cartland is a particular favourite, each book a centimetre thick and in slightly larger print than the others.

Today she brought us some kueh salat, a layer of sticky glutinous rice, slightly salty and rich with coconut milk beneath a green layer of sweet and creamy coconut custard infused with pandan.

'Wah!!!' enthused Auntie Fong. 'Jin ho jiak!'

'Mmmm!!!' I could only moan as my mouth was too full but I gave her an enthusiastic thumbs up.

Mrs Koh waved off the compliments, laughing. 'My grandson really likes my kueh salat so I made one whole dulang.'

I dashed off to wash my sticky fingers as the aunties were talking. By the time I came back, Mrs Koh was browsing the shelves and Auntie Fong went to wash her hands.

As I totted up the returns, an envelope fell out of a book.

'Mrs Koh, your letter.' I picked it up and brought it to her. She looked at it quizzically and said 'Not mine. It was already in the book when I bought it.'

'Unh,' I nodded going back to the cash register. I propped the envelope up against the lucky cat on the counter and went back to totting up the returns.

When Auntie Fong came back, she picked up the envelope.

'Who's Mary Wong ah?' she asked, opening the unsealed flap and pulling out a sheet of lined paper and a photograph. She put down the photo as she read the letter.

'Wah, you so kaypoh one,' commented Mrs Koh.

Auntie Fong ignored her and picked up the photo. 'Eh, Mei! Look at this girl — she's the one in the newspaper, right?'

Sally Song and Yock Li smiled up at me from the photograph. The two girls in their school uniforms stood in front of what looked like the school's bulletin board, arms crossed, back to back with their heads turned to look at the camera. I took the letter from Auntie Fong and read it, Mrs Koh craning over my shoulder.

'Hah! This kind of father also got,' she said disgustedly, flicking a tear from the corner of her eye.

'I think we'd better pass it to the police. Auntie Fong ah, maybe you can give it to Teck Wai tonight? I'll pass to you later, okay?'

After the lunch crowd, I brought the letter and photo over to Richard's little photo and copier shop. It was his uncle's shop but Richard ran it now. As usual, he was on his computer. In his polo with the shop's logo and jeans, he looked like a university student part-timing.

'Richard, I have a question. Can you make a copy of this photo?' I put it down in front of him. He pushed up his glasses, picked it up and looked at it dubiously.

'No film cannot.'

'You're so clever, can find a way, right?' I coaxed.

'Not so easy leh'

'But can, right?'

He rolled his eyes. Richard was in my class in Sec 4 and I know a little secret … well, actually everybody knows that little secret except maybe Maggie.

'How much?'

'$15.00.'

'What??? So ex one!'

I managed to haggle the price down to $5 for two copies of the photo with a photocopy or two thrown in. And still had time to go eat a late lunch. Love is a wonderful thing.

I went back to Richard's at around 5 pm to collect the photo and its copies. A quick zap or three and I also had copies of the letter.

'Thank you, Richard!' I sang as I handed him the $5 bill.

'You always one!' he grumbled as he took the money. 'People doing business here, you know? Don' play play, can or not.'

'I know, I know. Eh! What are you doing Sunday night? We're meeting up for dinner at Apolo, about 7.30. Come lah!'

Richard fussed a bit with the stuff on the counter, then nodded.

'I meet you here then we go, okay?'

On my way back to the shop, I swung by Jaipur Carpets.

'Uncle Nathan! Do you think Lakshmi's up for ice cream? I want to go to Swensen's to have ice cream and I'm looking for kaki.'

He laughed. 'The day my daughter doesn't want ice cream, I think the sky will fall down. I'll let her know you were looking for her.'

'I know, right? That's why I want to ask her. Nowadays, everybody is on diet! Oh, Auntie Rosnah! How about Nik? Can he come? The more the merrier.'

'Ya, I'll let him know.'

* * *

I passed the originals to Auntie Fong before I tucked the new photos and photocopies into the folder I keep in my bag.

'What's that?' she asked, taking the originals.

'Just copies.' I took them out of the folder and showed them to her.

'You made copies for what?'

'You see that second girl?' I pointed her out in the photo. 'Lakshmi brought her to Auntie Geok's after they announced that Sally died. Wah, her eyes all red! Must have been crying like anything. So I thought that maybe she wanted.'

'Then the other photo how? And the letter?' Her eyes drilled into me and I blushed a bit.

'Err ... since I was making a copy, I thought maybe make

two then ...' I trailed off trying to think of a reasonable excuse.

Auntie Fong snorted. 'Cheh! You always say I kaypoh, you also kaypoh! Two times! See other people, never see yourself.'

I laughed a bit sheepishly but couldn't think of a comeback.

1 Mar | Saturday

On Saturday, I met up with Nik and Lakshmi at 4 pm at Swensen's. I'd gotten there a bit early so I was already sitting at a table reading when they showed up. I only realised they had arrived when they jumped me from behind.

'What are you reading?' asked Lakshmi as she tried to take the book from me. I fended her off as I slipped in an old receipt to mark my page before I surrendered it to her. She took it and dropped into the chair next to mine.

She was wearing a nice dress which told me that she'd come from her parents' shop; they were very strict about her looking presentable when she was there. Her long wavy hair was twisted and messily clipped at the top of her head, off her neck.

'Good or not?' she asked as she read the back cover blurb.

'Pretty good. I haven't figured out who did it yet.'

'I can tell you now,' she grinned mischievously, pretending to look at the back page.

'Don't you dare!'

'Wah! So nice to be in aircon!' Nik sighed as he dumped his bag on the seat next to his. 'It's so hot outside.' He pulled a towel out of his bag and rubbed his face and hair vigorously.

His short curls were damp with sweat, even lightly dressed as he was in bermudas and short-sleeved t-shirt. After the rubbing, his face glowed.

'Where'd you come from?' I asked. There were a couple of black smudges on his khaki shorts.

'From my friend's place. We were working on his motorbike.'

'Who's this friend?'

'Ah, you won't know him — last time he was our neighbour but his family moved to Choa Chu Kang.'

'Oh, I see. So, what do you want to eat?' I pushed a menu towards him and Lakshmi immediately dropped my book to grab it. After a short pretend tug-of-war, they settled down to study the menu.

I studied their bent heads. The plan was to start by asking Lakshmi if she already knew what she wanted to study in university. But that could wait until they'd started on the ice cream.

Nik would have been happy with just a scoop of strawberry but the ice cream queen, Lakshmi, was determined to taste as many different flavours as she could and was trying to talk him into sharing an Earthquake. After much debate, we ordered an Earthquake for all three to share. Of course, with lashings of whipped cream, cherries, hot fudge, etc.

It came pretty quickly and we dug in.

'So did you tell Auntie Rosnah already?' asked Lakshmi. 'About the teacher's note.'

I silently blessed her for bringing up the subject but raised my eyebrows. 'Teacher's note?'

'The other day the teacher sent my mom a note,' Nik sighed. 'I haven't been doing very well in the quizzes.'

'Well, if you don't study ...' sniffed Lakshmi.

'It's so boring … and has nothing to do with what I want to do. What do I care what Canada's products are? It's got nothing to do with me!'

He actually has something he wants to do! I cheered inwardly.

'So, what do you want to do, Nik?' I asked, keeping my voice mildly interested.

'I've been working on my friend's motorbike and it's really cool! Everything fits and works together perfectly. That's what I want to do. It would be amazing to be able to build something new.'

'So … you want to become an engineer?'

'Ya …' he eyed me like I was an idiot. 'Of course.'

'Have you told your mother?'

'No …' he deflated. 'I don't want to worry her. We don't have the money to pay for me to go to university.'

'Did you even ask your mother?' Lakshmi asked.

'No, I don't want to upset her.'

'Nik, how do you know your mom doesn't have the money?' I asked.

'She's always saying how we have to save money … cannot waste … this cannot, that cannot …' He fiddled with his spoon despondently.

'Did it occur to you that she may be saving the money for your education?' I asked. Nik looked thunderstruck.

Lakshmi shook her head disgustedly. 'Goondu!'

'So … you couldn't be bothered to study since you didn't think you could study Engineering?'

Nik nodded mutely.

I looked at Lakshmi. 'Seriously short-term thinking.' She nodded vigorously.

'Nik, you need to talk to your mother about what you want to do. I'm sure she wants to do everything she can to help you but if you don't talk to her, how will she know what to do?' I frowned at him. 'Anyway, even if she can't afford it on her own, there are such things as scholarships and bursaries, you know. And then there's the polytechnic option.'

'Don't you need to have really good grades to get a scholarship?' he said dubiously.

'You can do it!' urged Lakshmi. 'You just need to work harder to catch up.'

Nik still looked unsure. I sat back and eyed him.

'Look, just talk to your mother soon, okay?' After a while, he rolled his eyes and nodded.

That settled, we focused on the ice cream for a bit. But I can't stay quiet, right?

'So, how's things at school?'

'Like that lah ...' Nik said, licking a drip off his hand.

'What about Sally? Any news?'

'No ... they're not telling us anything.' I looked at Lakshmi consideringly. She was inspecting her side of the Earthquake as though she was looking for a fly.

'Even if they're not telling you anything, is there something you know?' She flinched.

'How can she know anything? Sally was in my class not hers,' Nik pointed out. So competitive.

'So do you know something?' I asked Nik.

'Dam' bad luck, man. First she kena tekan then she gets

killed,' he shook his head sadly.

'Kena tekan? Nik, what's 'kena tekan' again?'

'Under pressure lah. Serious mugger, gets As and Bs ... so people not happy. Call her "nerd" la, "teacher's pet" la ...' He shook his head. 'That's not so bad but they also take her books and throw out the window. They throw one, she goes to get it then when she gets back they throw the next one.'

'What???' I was appalled. 'How come the teachers didn't stop it?'

'You think they do in front of the teacher?' he rolled his eyes. Of course, they never do it in front of the teachers.

'You never stopped them?'

He looked shamefaced. I was horrified. 'Don't tell me you were one of them?'

'No lah!' he exclaimed in horror. 'My mak would kill me.'

'So?'

He looked down then sighed. 'I didn't even try to stop them.'

I didn't need to ask him why. Get between bullies and their victims and you were likely to be their next target, as I knew very well. If it was a gang of them, it was guaranteed they would jump you. You just didn't know when.

Lakshmi sat open-mouthed for a while. Then her mouth snapped shut and she smacked Nik up the back of his head.

'Oi! No violence!' Nik said rubbing the offended spot. 'What would you have done?'

'Stop them, of course.' Lakshmi folded her arms, nose in the air.

'Eh! You think so easy, is it?'

'Ya.'

Nik eyed her then held up one finger. 'Me.'

Then he held up the other hand, all five fingers extended. 'Them. You think I got chance?'

Nothing wrong with Nik's instincts for survival. Much better than Lakshmi's. She would have charged in and suffered for it.

'You could have told the teacher ...' Her voice trailed off, self-righteousness gone. Even Lakshmi knew that was not going to happen. If Nik had told a teacher and it had gotten out, his name would have been mud and he'd have been the target of every pai kia and isolated by everyone else.

'So, who were the bullies, Nik?'

He gave me a narrow-eyed look. 'Why you want to know? You don't need to know.'

'What if it had something to do with Sally's dying?'

'Why would it have anything to do with her dying?'

'You stoopid, is it?' Lakshmi exclaimed. 'Of course it might. The police are asking all kinds of questions. They came to your class, they even came to my class!'

Nik digested this. He looked troubled but said nothing.

Lakshmi opened her mouth but I beat her to it.

'Lakshmi, what were you going to say when Nik so rudely interrupted?' I gave him a stern look and he grinned unrepentantly.

'I don't remember.'

'Can don't buat bodoh, can or not? If you don't want to say, I tell her for you.'

Immediately, Lakshmi said, 'I'll tell her.' Glaring at him then turning to me: 'I think Yock Li already knew that Sally was

54

dead.'

'I thought you said she was very upset when she heard? That's why you brought her to Auntie Geok's.'

'I know! I know! But I've been thinking about it and it seems like since Monday she was already …' Lakshmi paused to think. 'Very stress. Maybe sad?'

'Your imagination.' Nik scoffed. 'Think too hard.'

'She could have been sad because of a lot of things? Maybe they fought.' I offered.

By the time the ice cream was finished, we were all happy and maybe a bit hyper. I paid the bill. 'My treat!' I said, fingers crossed behind my back. 'Nik! Don't forget to talk to your mother, ya?'

Just as we were leaving, I remembered something.

'Lakshmi,' I said, digging in my bag. 'Can pass to Yock Li?' I handed her the photo in an envelope. 'I thought she might want this photo; she might not have a copy.'

2 Mar | Sunday

Even before she opened her shop, Auntie Rosnah came looking for me with a big smile.

'Thank you, sayang!' she cried, clasping me to her sky-blue tunic. Her tudung draped in graceful folds around her face and neck, was pinned in place with a sunburst.

'You're welcome.' I handed her the Swensen's bill and she paid me right there and then, her smile hardly dimming at all.

* * *

Nik and Lakshmi came by in the afternoon. Needless to say, Nik was beaming.

'So how?' I asked. 'What did your mom say?'

'Ya!' he said, punching the air. 'But I'm going to have to work hard because I need to up my grades.'

'Great! You think you can?'

'We're going to be studying together,' Lakshmi said. 'Starting now.' And she towed him off.

* * *

Banana Leaf Apolo was packed. Richard and I got there at

about 7.45 pm and goggled at the crowds outside the door. Luckily Shanti and Yong had gotten there early to chope a table big enough for all of us. Ah, the joys of a five-day working week.

We were the last there and crammed ourselves in at the ends, next to Maggie and Shanti. Of course, I made sure Richard was next to Maggie.

'Wah, Richard! Long time no see!' smiled Shanti. 'See, Yong, you're not the only thorn anymore. Don't complain so much.'

Yong, who was reacting melodramatically to Shanti's elbow in his ribs, grinned and reached across the table to shake Richard's hand.

'Ho seh! It's been a while, man!'

'Aiyah, what to do? Boh eng, neh …'

'Eh Mei, can switch?'

So I exchanged seats with Yong and watched resignedly as he and Richard caught up while Maggie was focused on Sharm's discourse on parent–teacher politics in school.

The waiter distributed the banana leaves then came back to dish out scoops of steaming hot rice onto the leaves while a second man ladled out helpings of vegetable dishes and dal. A third followed, handing out pappadums. Ooh, pappadums!! I immediately picked mine up and broke off a piece to pop into my mouth.

The dishes we'd ordered arrived: small plates of mutton curry, butter chicken and a big, deep dish of fish head curry. We all shut up and focused on eating.

The important thing to remember about eating a fish head is that the best parts of the fish head are not so easily accessible. It's all about the collar that lies between the pectoral fins and the gill cover, the delicate cheeks that you have to scoop out and the jelly like bits in the eyes.

Happily, in the group I was the only one to relish these treasures, so I didn't have to fight anyone for them. I scooped up some brinjal and lady's fingers onto my banana leaf and drizzled a ladle of the gravy over my rice then tucked in to savour every bite. Fish curry is the best, even when no head is involved.

When all there was left were empty plates and folded banana leaves, mine folded over a heap of fish bones, we chatted idly.

Sharm said dreamily, 'You know what? We should institute parent licences. Everybody who wants to have children should have to pass a certification exam to get a licence. Compulsory birth control until you get your licence to parent. Then if the offspring break rules, or are found to be troublesome pains in the behind, the parents get penalised on top of having to pay for any damages.'

Shanti laughed, 'That'd have all the religions up in arms! The Catholics, the Muslims ...'

'My parents would freak!' Maggie said. 'They'd picket Parliament.'

'Students giving you problems?' Yong asked Sharm sympathetically.

'Them and their parents! "How come my daughter didn't get A* in Science? She's very smart, you know, and works soooo hard!" Or "Why my son got detention yesterday? He's such a gooood boy!" Our time, it was "What? You got detention, is it? Serves you right! Next time don't be so naughty!" Remember?'

Yong grinned. 'My uncle complains that we've got it too easy these days. Apparently when he gets a new batch of NS boys, he also gets inundated with calls and visits from mothers with instructions on how to look after their precious babies.'

'Sharm, you're teaching in Alexandra Secondary School, right? You ever teach the girl that was killed?'

'Ummm ... maybe? I don't remember.'

I looked at her disapprovingly.

'What? Don't look at me like that. With sixty kids in each class, it's hard to differentiate them. If her parents didn't come and harass me about anything ... sounds bad, right?'

'Wow, sixty kids in one class?' I tried to imagine myself standing in front of a class of 60. 'Were there that many when we were in school?'

'No ... in our time only got about thirty, thirty-five.' Wow ... almost doubled. No wonder.

'Has the school said anything about what happened to her?'

'Actually, no leh. They just told us to watch out for any students who seem traumatised by the event, and to direct any enquiries to the head's office. Like we're so free.' Sharm sniffed.

'That's all, huh.' I chewed on that. Seems like the school was just moving on from Sally's death. Not that I could think of anything else they could do, considering. But even so ...

'What are you thinking about?' Shanti asked, rapping the table in front of me.

'Huh?' I jumped, jerked back into the moment. 'Nothing. It just seems a bit sad that a girl is dead and everybody is just moving on without her.'

'What do you expect them to do?'

I sighed. 'I don't know. It just seems like nobody cares. It's sad.'

I looked around the crowded restaurant. Tables of families, others occupied by friends, eating, talking and laughing together. Everybody dies alone, but the fact that Sally seems to have lived alone and unsupported seemed to be unutterably sad. Deserted by her mother, ignored by her father, having to find her way on her own. Would it have been better if she had been an orphan cast on the mercies of the gahmen?

3 Mar | Monday

Yock Li showed up at Auntie Geok's shop in the afternoon. She stood there looking around and then saw me shelving books over the way.

'Thanks for the photo! But how did you get it?'

'Oh, it's just a copy. We found it in a letter in a book that was returned. I thought you might like it.'

'What about the letter?'

'The letter? What about it?' Shouldn't have mentioned the letter.

'Who was it to?' Why was she so interested?

'It was to her mother.'

'What did it say?'

I put down my stack of books and came out to join her. I didn't want to tell her what the letter said — it was too personal and I really didn't think that it was any of her business. But ... maybe she could tell me more about Sally.

'I don't know. I didn't read it.'

'If you didn't read it, how do you know it was to her mother?'

'It was addressed to her on the envelope.'

Yock Li looked frustrated. She thought I was lying but couldn't just come out and call me a liar. What if I got mad?

'So how did you know there was a photo inside? How did

you get it out? You must have opened the envelope, right?'

'The envelope wasn't sealed. But just because I opened the envelope doesn't mean I read the letter. I'm not that kaypoh.' Liar, liar, pants on fire.

'So, what did you do with it?'

'I mailed it, of course.'

'But Sally didn't know where her mother was.'

'And how do you know that?'

She opened her mouth and paused.

'She told me.'

'You must have been very close,' I said gently. 'I'm so sorry for your loss.'

She gave me a startled look then tried to look like she didn't care but soon her lower lip began to tremble.

'She — she missed her mother so much.' Yock Li bit her lip. 'Her father doesn't — didn't really care about her. He's never at home, he never gave her money for school things, not even for food! She had to earn money just to eat.'

'That's so terrible! Where was she working?'

Tears gathered in her eyes and she opened her mouth … then closed it again. She swiped at her eyes.

'I … don't know. I've got to go. Thanks again for the photo.' She gathered herself together abruptly and walked off. I watched her go.

'What did you say to her?'

The harsh whisper made me jump. I turned to see Third Girl standing at my shoulder, watching Yock Li. Where did she come from? She wasn't anywhere in sight just a moment ago!

'What?'

'What did you say to her?' Third Girl glared at me. 'Why is she so upset? Were you asking her about Sally?'

'Why do you think so? Do you know something?'

'Sally was a nuisance to everyone. To me, to Yock Li, everyone!'

'How did you get from you and Yock Li to "everyone"?' I asked interestedly. 'And how was she a nuisance to Yock Li? Seems like she is more upset than anyone about Sally.'

'Urrgh!' she growled. Uh oh, she looked pretty mad. And even though she was only average sized, that still made her bigger than I was.

She reached out to grab my shoulders, possibly to shake me. Since she was bigger than me, I backed away. 'Oi! You know got such thing as "personal space" or not?'

She kept coming. I kept backing.

'Why are you so mad? You know she came to see me, right? It's not like I went to her!'

'Si mi tai ji?' Auntie Fong had showed up just in time. Great! Back-up!

'Just stay away from her!' Third Girl backed away jabbing a finger at me. Very rudely, I must say. Ma would have smacked my hand if I'd done that.

'Wah!' Auntie Fong turned to me. 'Nowadays very exciting one ah?'

* * *

Even though I had already accepted the NIE offer, I still wasn't sure if that was what I wanted to do for a living.

'Teaching is a very fulfilling occupation,' I told myself as I washed the plates.

'You'll be developing the next generation of leaders!' I said as I wiped the counters.

I slumped down on the sofa.

'You'll be repeating the same damn thing for the next twenty years if you live that long!'

I sighed and pushed myself up. 'Ma! Ah Pa! I'm going to the hawker centre.'

Ma came out of the bedroom drying her hair. 'So late already, you want to go out!'

Her hair's getting white around the roots. Time to colour.

'Aiyaa, don't worry lah. I'm big already.' I gave her a bear hug. 'See?'

I'm bigger than my mother, although not by much, and my dad's not much bigger than I am. Both of them were stunted by malnutrition like many people born during and in the years after World War II. Beng is practically a giant by comparison at 170 cm and Ling is not bad at 160 cm but I'm barely 150 cm! It's very unfair.

'You ah!' she batted at me, trying not to smile.

As I was walking down the stairs, my pager vibrated. Auntie Fong's home number? Wondering what happened, I stopped at the cardphone in the void deck.

'Hello?' A man's voice; must be Teck Wai.

'Teck Wai ah? This is Mei. Your mother paged me.'

'No, I was the one who paged you.'

'Oh ... what's up?'

'Well ... wait, are you at home?'

'No, I'm on my way to the hawker centre.'

'Which one? I'll meet you there.'

'West Coast Market.'

'Set. I'll be there in fifteen minutes. Meet you where?'

'How about the mamak stall facing the road? Near the bus stop.'

'Okay.' He rang off and I hung up wondering.

* * *

I was sitting with my teh tarik facing the bus stop so I could see him coming but he surprised me by coming from the other direction.

'Eeks!' I jumped as he sat down beside me. 'Why did you come this way? Didn't you take the bus?'

'I drove.' He popped up again and went to buy a drink.

His hair was still damp, so I guess he'd just had a shower and he was wearing brightly patterned board shorts topped with a university t-shirt that had seen better days and sandals; a world away from his office wear. He came back with it and sat across the table from me. The scent of tea and ginger wafted up.

'Wah! Got car already ah? So big shot one!'

'Have to lah. Any time also kena call.'

'So ... why so free today?'

'Off duty.'

'Oh ...'

'Oh ya, thanks for the letter and photo!'

'So how? Have you caught the killer yet?'

'No lah, not yet.' He took a sip of his teh halia and his

glasses fogged. He took them off and polished them with his t-shirt. 'Siong ah! Nobody saw her, nobody knows why she was there. Buay tahan.' He rolled his eyes and put his glasses on again.

'Her father also useless. Act blur only. He says he didn't even know she was out that night.'

'Hmm ... one of her school friends told me he really boh hew her. Didn't even give her money to buy food.'

'Hah? Like that ah? If she wasn't dead I'd report him to Child Protective Services.' He did a double take. 'Wait, what's her friend's name? I tell you — nobody would say anything. Maybe if I zero in on the friend, she'll tell me a bit more.'

'Yock Li. Actually she's the other girl in the photo. Sorry, don't know her family name or how to spell. If you want, I can ask Lakshmi.'

'Ya, please.' He pulled out a notebook and pen from his back pocket and made a note.

I looked at his bent head. Don't try, won't know, right?

'How did she die?' I asked quietly, leaning close to him.

His head jerked up and he eyed me disapprovingly.

'Wah, so kaypoh one.'

'Come on ... I'm helping, right? I promise I won't tell anyone,' I said wheedlingly. He gave me the eye. I sat still and looked as trustworthy as I could. 'Come on, Teck Wai,' I silently urged. 'Give a bit, lah.'

Finally he sighed and leaned forward. 'She was suffocated,' he whispered then, his warm breath tickling my ear. 'You better don't tell anyone.'

'Cross my heart and hope to die!' I said, crossing a big X

over my heart.

He grunted and put away his notebook.

'So how come you're down here so late?'

'It's only nine o'clock! I just … needed to jalan-jalan a bit.'

'If you want I can take you for a drive.'

'Ooh … Can!' I downed the rest of my tea and smiled, 'Please!'

* * *

'Wah!!!' I slid into the passenger seat of the blue car. 'So cute! What kind of car is it?'

'A Suzuki Swift GTI. I bought it last year. Wah! The COE damn jialat. More expensive than the car!'

He started the car and drove out of the parking lot. 'So how? Where do you want to go?'

'Anywhere. Just drive around also can.'

He pulled out into the road.

'So, my mom says you're starting NIE, is it?'

'Yaa … I guess …'

He laughed. 'Wah! You sound so enthusiastic.'

I groaned and looked out the window. 'I really can't see myself as a teacher.'

'At least got job.'

'Wah lau! You sound just like my father!'

He drove along West Coast Road in silence for a bit.

'So how do you like your job?'

'Interesting — a lot to learn.'

'Inspector Rizwan seems nice. Very patient.'

'He's very garang but he knows a lot so not bad.'

I sighed. 'Maybe I should join the police instead.'

'You? Siao! I can just see you on patrol. Small little girl chasing a tua chiak!' He sniggered.

'Umf!' I slid down in the seat and stared out the window.

We crossed Clementi Road into Pasir Panjang. In the light of the streetlamps, I could see the shuttered doors of the shophouses.

Somewhere on the other side of the shophouses was NUS, my stomping ground just a couple of years ago. Somehow it seemed like an age away. Those were the days … wait a minute! Wasn't I a bit too young to be getting all nostalgic about the days of my youth? I guess this whole thing about going to NIE was getting to me.

As we passed the shophouses at the corner of Pasir Panjang and South Buona Vista, the bars were still going strong.

Teck Wai turned left on to South Buona Vista. My favourite duck rice shop was still open, brightly lit and still packed. I had fond memories of skipping class to rush over there early so we could beat the lunch hour crowd. Tender slices of braised duck with lashings of homemade fried chilli, not to mention the tofu that had been soaking in the braising liquid until it had soaked up all the flavour. Yum … maybe I could come for lunch on my next afternoon off.

Then Teck Wai turned off the road onto Vigilante Drive. The streetlights partially illuminated the occasional cluster of trees and as the car's headlights swept around bends, it flickered across tree trunks and I thought I saw a flash of reflecting animal eyes.

He parked the car and then got out. Hmm … if he wasn't Auntie Fong's son I'd be worried. A man and a woman alone in an isolated location … the beginning of many a murder mystery.

Then he stuck his head back in.

'Coming or not?' he asked.

'I hope you're not planning to do something like go trekking at this hour of night.'

'Don't be silly. You said you wanted to jalan-jalan, right? So, let's go jalan-jalan.'

I got out of the car and followed him to the start of the foot path. Although there were a couple of cars parked, there was no one in sight. We strolled around, listening to the crickets and the quiet sounds of the nightlife. In the distance we could see the sky lit by the bright lights of Pasir Panjang Terminal.

As we ambled about in companionable silence, I could feel my restlessness seep away to be replaced by the serenity of the park. It was nice not to have to talk.

Eventually we returned to the car but as we were getting in, I suddenly remembered something.

'Teck Wai, did Sally's mother contact you after the sketch came out in the newspapers?'

'No, why?'

'It seems like nobody knows where she is. I thought that if she saw the sketch, she would have come forward.'

'Maybe she doesn't read the papers?'

'Or maybe she's also dead.'

'Eh, I checked the records already and nobody reported her missing, okay?'

'Just because nobody reported her missing doesn't mean

she's not. If nobody hears a tree fall in the jungle, it doesn't mean it didn't fall.'

'It doesn't mean it did either!'

'So, I'll report her missing then.'

'You don't even know her! Can don't be so kaypoh, can or not?'

And that was the end of it. Not another word was said until Teck Wai pulled up at my block.

'Thanks for the drive and the walk,' I said a little stiffly as I got out.

'No prob — don't forget to ask Lakshmi for the name, ya?'

'Okay.' I headed up the staircase.

As I turned on the landing, I saw him still watching and made shooing motions for him to go. And he did.

4 Mar | Tuesday

'Mei.'

'Just a minute.'

I finished taping up the book cover, smoothing the tape down with the back of the stapler to make sure it stuck smoothly and well. Some people are so careless. Its cover had almost been completely torn off when it was returned. I opened and closed it to check that all was secure before finally looking up at Lakshmi.

'Oh, hi!'

'Wah, you really like books!' Lakshmi smiled as she looked down at me over the counter.

'Huh?' I looked down to see my hand still stroking the book that lay beneath it. 'I guess I do. Books contain so much, ideas, information, entertainment … you name it.'

Lakshmi sighed.

'What's up?'

'I just feel bad about Sally. I didn't know she was being bullied. And then to die like that …'

'Nothing you could have done.' I said brusquely. And that was true. If she had tried to interfere, they would have turned on her.

'But —'

I sighed. She really wasn't going to let it go. What was I

going to do with her?

'Look, just drop it. If you do something or say something to them, they are going to turn on you and I really don't want that for you. It's not fun.'

She looked stunned, her mouth forming a silent 'Oh'.

'Mei, were you bullied?'

'They tried,' I said grimly.

'What did you do?'

'I survived.' She went from stunned to horrified. 'Don't look like that lah! What doesn't kill me only makes me stronger.' I bared my teeth in a ferocious grimace and flexed my muscles. 'See? Stronger!' Her answering smile was weak so I changed the subject to something that had been on my mind since Saturday.

'Anyway, how's Nik getting on?'

'Okay lah! Mostly. His Geography sucks.'

'He doesn't need Geography to do Engineering.'

'He needs Geography to pass his O-levels.'

'Tell him to work harder.' I paused, then decided to address it headlong. 'Anyway, I was wondering … can you tell me Yock Li's full name?'

'Why?'

Aiyo! Why do I always get this answer when I ask for info? Is it because it's real life or because it's Singapore?

'Wah! You act like it's a big secret. I cannot be kaypoh, is it?'

She cocked her head to one side and grinned mischievously. 'So, how much should I charge for the information?' She put a finger to her cheek and went 'Mmmm …'

Well, two can play that game!

'So, what have you been up to recently that I should tell

your parents?' I put a finger to my cheek and went 'Hmmm ...'

'You wouldn't!'

I didn't even dignify that with an answer, just folded my arms and rolled my eyes.

'Okay! Okay!' She surrendered. 'Umm ... it's Tan.'

'Can write the whole name down for me?'

* * *

'Teck Wai? Her name is Tan Yock Li. Y-O-C-K space L-I.'

* * *

After dinner I opened my working folder. I'd made a few additional copies of Sally's letter. After all, at ten cents a copy, it would hardly bankrupt me ... and might come in useful. But I wasn't quite sure how yet.

> *Ma,*
>
> *Where are you? I went to Crest Motors to see you but they say you're not there any more. Why you never tell me?*
>
> *The uncle at the gate wouldn't let me in so I asked him to call you for me but he said your name is not on the list.*
>
> *How can? I said he never look properly. But he said don't have. Finally he called HR and the woman told me you left two months ago. Two months! How come you never say? The woman also said she doesn't know*

where you went.

Why did you go like that? Where did you go? I want to go with you! I don't want to stay here with Pa!

He is getting worse and worse. I don't want to call him 'Pa' any more. I won't call him 'Pa' any more. He's not like a father at all. First he said I need to pay everything myself 'cos he can't find a job. So I take part-time jobs, I earn money to pay for my food. I even have to pay for utilities sometimes but when he wants, he just comes and takes all my money.

Now he says I don't earn enough, that I should go look for job down in Geylang.

What to do, Ma? I can't take it anymore. Can I come live with you?

Please let me live with you!

Even if you only have a room! I won't take much space. I can sleep on the floor. I don't have much and I'm not very big.

Please, Ma! Look at the photo — don't you want to see me? I want to see you so much!

Sally

So poor thing. There were faint streaks and smudges on the copies that I hadn't noticed on the letter itself. Were they invisible tearstains on the original letter rendered visible by the magic of zapping or just the result of a dirty photocopier glass?

I couldn't imagine being in her position; with no one to depend on, she was effectively an abandoned child. My eyes started to prickle as they filled with tears. Damn! I hate crying so easily.

I really wanted to beat up that father of hers. Such a bastard. Even her mother. How could she disappear without telling her daughter? Where did she go? When did she go? The letter wasn't dated. So many questions.

Actually … Crest Motors is on Pandan Crescent and that is really nearby — I could even walk. The only question was how to get the guard to let me in and get people to talk to me.

I rested my chin on my hands and considered.

Agatha Christie's *They Came to Baghdad* came to mind. If Victoria Jones could fake it all the way to Baghdad as Victoria Pauncefoot Jones, the niece of a famous archaeologist, surely I could fake my way past a security guard.

I could already hear Shanti's voice saying 'Oi Mei! Since when do you live in an Agatha Christie novel? You think the guard so stupid, is it?'

Oh well. Don't try, won't know, right?

5 Mar | Wednesday

After I got back from work, I checked my good shoes then dressed carefully in my interview outfit. I picked up the folder I'd prepared last night and slung The Bag over my shoulder. I nodded at the girl in the mirror. She looked exactly like a fresh grad applying for a job.

As luck would have it, Ma was coming out of the kitchen as I was unlocking the gate.

'Eh, where are you going? Got interview, is it? You got apply for a job, is it? How come never say?'

'No, no. I'm just going out for a while.'

'Why dress until like that?'

'Why not?'

She rolled her eyes and I escaped.

The walk to Crest Motors was hot, but bearable with my umbrella up. I stopped by the guardhouse and signed in, citing HR as who I was visiting and submission of application as my reason. I must have looked suitably nervous and sweaty. The guard let me through without comment.

When I walked into the reception area, the first thing I saw was a counter behind which a few men in blue shirts worked at their desks. A big bespectacled man with a red face came to the counter but just then a woman came from the staircase and hailed me. She was an older woman with crisp permed curls and brutally plucked eyebrows. A pair of glasses hung on a chain around her neck.

'Miss Tang?'

'Yes!'

'I'm Mrs Tan. Please follow me.'

She led me up the stairs to an open office where a number of people were working diligently. On one side, a door stood open and she led me through it into a meeting room then closed the door behind us.

'Please sit down,' she said and seated herself as well. 'Is that your CV?' She held out her hand and I handed her the folder.

She opened it and paused. 'What's this?'

Instead of the CV she expected, there was only a copy of Sally's letter.

'I'm sorry but I lied to the guard. I'm actually trying to find Mary Wong.'

She sniffed. 'I was rather surprised to hear that somebody had come to hand in an application since we hadn't advertised any positions. Why are you trying to find her?'

'Her daughter is dead.'

'What?' Her eyes widened then narrowed. 'What's that got to do with you? Or me.'

'I saw her just before she died. And then I found that letter. Once I read it …' I stopped, unable to articulate just how it had affected me.

She cast me a sharp glance then put on her glasses and started to read. Her stern face gave little away as she read but I thought it had softened a little by the time she put down the letter.

She took off her glasses and rubbed the bridge of her nose.

'I don't remember talking to the girl. But if she came two months after Mary ... wait here.' She got up and left, coming back about ten minutes later with a paper folder. Seating herself back down, she opened it and ran her finger down the first page.

'If she heard that Mary Wong had left two months before, then she would have come in ... July last year.'

'So, she left in May? Did she say where she was going?'

'No, she did not.' Mrs Tan hesitated then, weighing her words carefully, added 'In fact, she never even told us she was going to leave.'

The words didn't register at first.

'You mean she never resigned?'

'No, she didn't. She came in to work as usual one day and didn't the next. No call, no letter. We tried calling her home number but she wasn't there and her landlord hadn't seen her either.'

'So ...'

'I tried to reach her a few more times with no success. Finally we sent her a registered letter of termination. It came back two weeks later.'

I slumped back in my chair.

'Did you report her missing?'

'Miss Tang, I am not her keeper,' Mrs Tan said coldly. 'She was an adult with the right to come and go as she pleased.'

'But ...' I saw her face and changed what I was about to say. 'Does anybody have any idea what happened to her?'

She waved a hand. 'Oh, there was a lot of gossip. Someone said she had run away with a man, another that her husband must have killed her — that kind of thing.'

'I see.' I chewed on that.

'If that is all …' She closed her folder and stood up. My time was up.

'Is there any chance you could give me her address?' I asked as I put the copy back into my folder.

'Young lady,' her voice was so chilly I had goosebumps. 'That information is confidential.'

I didn't argue. Hurriedly I tore yet another page out of my notebook and wrote down my name and pager number. Maybe I should have name cards made.

'If that's the case, would it be possible to file this in Mary's folder? If she contacts you, could you ask her to page me?'

She looked at the paper a while, then took it and stuck it in the folder.

'If I'm still here. If I remember.'

'That's all I'm asking.'

* * *

'You what?' spluttered Shanti.

We were back in the hawker centre having our usuals.

'I went to Crest Motors to see if I could find Sally's mother.' I sighed and stirred my chendol. 'But no luck. She didn't even give notice. Just disappeared.'

'I can't believe you even managed to persuade the HR person to talk to you!' Shanti said half disbelieving, half admiring.

'I'm lucky she was curious.'

'So, are you done? No more kaypohing?'

'Ummm … I suppose. Do you think it's a coincidence that the mother disappeared and then the daughter was killed?'

'Mei, the girl was murdered. Has it occurred to you that poking your nose around her life could get dangerous?'

'Where do you think Mary Wong is? I wonder why she left so suddenly.'

Did Mr Song know where his wife — wait a minute; were they still married or divorced?

A sudden clap right in front of my face made me jump.

Shanti was glaring at me.

'Now that I have your attention, what was the last thing I said?'

'Err …' I racked my brain desperately and came up with nothing. 'Sorry …' I said humbly. 'What did you say?'

'I asked you,' she said in long-suffering tones, 'if it had occurred to you that poking around Sally's life could get dangerous. She was murdered, you know!' That last was loud enough that heads around us turned at the word 'murdered'.

I hurriedly shushed her. 'Yes, yes, of course I know that.'

'I think you should just stop your kaypohing. What if someone comes after you?'

'Nobody's going to come after me.'

'You think nobody's going to come after you?' Shanti smacked her brow. 'Have we been reading the same murder mysteries? In the ones I read, the killer always comes after the one who's been kaypohing. And you've been leaving your name and number everywhere!'

'Okay, okay … I see where you're coming from. But really, I'm only speaking to people who knew Sally or her mother, you know, like Nik and Lakshmi and Sharm's colleagues. I just want to find out a bit more about her. It's not like I'm trying to break into locked rooms or anything.'

'Hmf!' she sniffed. 'If you had any idea where there was a secret, you'd be breaking in there without a second thought. You're like a cross between a rottweiler and a chihuahua.'

'A chihuahua?' I cried, offended.

'Or maybe a bloodhound and a mule? You know, nosy and stubborn,' she mused.

I was speechless.

6 Mar | Thursday

'Mei, how do you stop people from saying nasty things?' Lakshmi's voice was troubled.

'About you?' I looked up at her. As usual she was draped over the counter. Auntie Fong would scold her about being spineless but she was out on her tea break.

'Noo …'

'What happened?'

'Everybody's been guessing like mad about how Sally died. I mean, who knows, right? The newspapers never say anything, the teachers never say anything …'

'And nature abhors a vacuum …' I nodded. 'So, what were they saying?'

'All kinds of things lah! It was a teacher, it was a jealous boyfriend, it was drugs — some said she was a drug addict and the dealer killed her because she didn't pay, another lot said she was selling drugs and it was the drug addict that killed her.'

'Oh no!'

'The latest one is that Sally was a prostitute … and that it was one of her customers who killed her.'

'What???' Did she actually go ahead and do it? In her letter it didn't seem like she would but if that letter was written more than six months ago, could she have become desperate enough?

'When Yock Li heard that one, she freaked out. Started screaming at the guy who said it. Luckily I managed to catch her in time. She was going to go for him.'

'So how?'

'A teacher came in and broke it up. But since then, she's gotten more and more angry. I think if it goes on, she's going to blow up.'

'Aiyo!' was all I could think of to say. What to do? There was no way Lakshmi could stop the gossip; I don't think anybody could. Not for nothing did Agatha Christie liken the rumours to the Lernean Hydra in the Labours of Hercules, cut off one head and two grow in its place. The only way would be to replace it with something even more startling and gossip worthy ... or to find out what really happened.

'Isn't her friend helping?'

'Her friend?'

'That girl who came along when you brought her the other day.'

'You mean Chloe?'

'Oh, her name is Chloe, is it?'

'Chloe Teng.' Lakshmi straightened up and snorted. 'She's one of the people starting all the rumours. Can't stand her. In front of Yock Li, she's all sympathetic. Behind her back, she says all kinds of things. Really two-faced.' She waved her hand dismissively. 'But what to do, Mei?'

'Other than being there for Yock Li and keeping her out of trouble, I really don't know what more you can do. You can't stop people from talking. Telling a teacher also no point — they also can't do anything and you will make yourself a target. Until the police find out who killed Sally, it's not going to stop.'

Lakshmi slumped back down. 'That's going to be never!!!!' she wailed.

7 Mar | Friday

I was standing outside the shop tidying the children's books display, bopping and singing along to 'Macarena', which Matt was playing next door so I nearly jumped out of my skin when Sharm grabbed me.

'You!' I scolded batting at her. 'What are you doing here?'

She grabbed my other hand and swung me around. 'It's Friday so we're celebrating.'

As we spun, I saw that she wasn't alone. Three more people stood smiling at me. Fellow teachers?

'Good for you.' I smiled them. 'Where are you going?'

'Cha Cha Cha,' said the other woman in the group. 'The plan is to order jugs of margaritas and get drunk.' She was striking in a draped, deep-blue dress under a brightly patterned kimono jacket, beautifully made-up with full red lips and long hair that was messily piled at the top of her head and skewered with what looked like a red pen.

'Hmm … I prefer my margaritas frozen,' commented the taller of the two men. His words were tinged with an American accent.

'Well, you can buy your own,' Sharm said decidedly. 'Or we could get a jug of frozen … Do they do jugs of frozen margarita?'

'How much are you planning on drinking tonight?' he

asked. 'I have to drive home, you know. So I probably won't be drinking much. And I'm sure some of us have ECA tomorrow.'

'You so no fun one,' grumped Red Lips.

The other man tsked and shook his head at her. 'Language! Lucky no students around to hear you.' Shorter than American Accent, his hair was long enough to curl and he wore glasses with black rectangular frames which gave his narrow face a studious look.

'Why don't you ever shave?' Red Lips replied, pointedly referencing his heavily stubbled jaw line.

'Oh, but I do shave! Every day, just like you.'

I managed to swallow my appalled laugh. Ooh ... that was nasty!

She smirked. 'I know you need keep cool but you really should use the razor on your face as well.' It was starting to feel like a pingpong match. One all, I think.

'Don't worry about it,' Sharm said. 'They actually get along. They just like to chochok each other.'

'We're keeping score,' said Red Lips. 'I'm winning.'

'No, you're not!'

'Ooh! Why don't we bring Mei along?' Sharm said hastily. 'She can help drink the margaritas.'

'Can.' said Red Lips. 'She can also help balance the group. I'm feeling outnumbered here.' Eh? Really? Two men, two women, how can it be unbalanced?

'My dear Yi Ling,' said American Accent. 'Even if it was just you against an army of men, I doubt you'd be outnumbered.'

She wrinkled her nose at him. 'Thanks for the compliment ... I think.'

'Great idea! The more the merrier,' said Mr Stubble. Then, turning to me, he added, 'Don't worry, we're really quite nice people, you know.' He smiled down at me. I smiled back but shook my head.

'Thanks but I'm still —'

'Go! Go!' Auntie Fong cried from inside the shop. She came out carrying The Bag.

'But —'

'Hai ya! What? You think I can't close by myself, is it?' She pushed The Bag into my arms, swung me around and gave me a small push.

'Okay, okay. Thanks, Auntie!' I laughed, slipping The Bag onto my shoulder as I turned to Sharm. 'Shall we go?'

'Let's go!' Sharm urged her group. 'Oh! I forgot to introduce you to everyone!' She pointed at Mr Stubble. 'That's Jeevan. Teaches Biology and Science.' Indicating American Accent: 'John — English and Literature. And this is Yi Ling who teaches Art and Design. Everybody, this is Mei, my classmate from school.'

I smiled and waved.

As we passed the public phone on the counter in the lobby, I stopped to let Ma know that I wouldn't be home for dinner. Sharm waited for me and fell in step as we walked along some way behind the others.

'Why this sudden urge to go out?' I asked. 'You always say Friday night is your time to sleep.'

'This past week has been horrible,' she sighed. 'I guess the police haven't found any leads so they keep coming back to question the students more intensively. The teachers too. Makes us feel like maybe one of us killed her. So, everyone is feeling …

stressed.'

'Oh no …'

'Anyway, we were sitting in the staff room moaning about it when someone suggested we have a night out to forget our problems. So here we are!'

* * *

We were early enough that we managed to get a table at Cha Cha Cha, just in front of the kitchen; a good thing, according Sharm, as it reduced the chances of them being seen by a passing parent or student. I found myself sitting in the middle of the banquette, squeezed in between Sharm and Yi Ling, while the men sat facing us.

Big bowls of tortilla chips and little bowls of salsa came, rapidly followed by the jugs of margarita. Soon we were pretty happy and greeted the last of the party merrily when he turned up.

The latecomer took the last chair, across from Sharm. The tallest of the group, he was also the most crumpled of them, his shirt having freed itself from his pants at the back and his sleeves escaping from the roll-up. His spectacles seemed to have had an accident, one hinge being held together with tape.

He reached a hand across the table to shake mine.

'Hi, I'm Yi Wei.'

'I'm Mei. What happened to your glasses?'

'His wife caught him with another woman and whacked him!' said Sharm gleefully.

'Really?' I asked, eyes wide, and his ears turned red.

'No lah! You all aaa … really,' he said crossly. 'If I were married, I wouldn't be here with this bunch of jokers.'

'Aww … don't be mad. You know you love us, man!' John laughed. Turning to me he said, 'He got in the way of a volleyball while the girls were practising this afternoon.'

Sharm shook her head at him. 'You really should keep your eyes open when you're near them. Some of their spikes are downright scary, even after they bounce.'

'Ya boy! That's what got me.'

'What were you doing there?'

'I was checking the sound system in the hall.' He grinned sheepishly. 'What to do? That was the only free time I had.'

'So how long have you been working at Can-Do?' asked John, who sat across from me.

'About eight months?' I did a quick count on my fingers to confirm.

'Do you enjoy it?'

'Of course!' What was there not to like? As jobs went, it couldn't get much better … except maybe paywise. Auntie Fong was reasonable and treated me like a favourite niece. I got to read any book I liked — even take them home overnight to finish.

'Huh,' laughed Sharm. 'You might say she's in heaven, working in a bookshop. It's hard to pull her nose out of a book. Even before uni.'

'Really? What did you study? Not Maths, I suppose.' John grinned. I guess he hadn't missed the finger counting.

'English Lit.'

'Ooh! My kind of guy — I mean girl! What do you read?'

'These days? Mainly murder.' Oops! Even I could feel the

mood drop at the mention of the word.

Sharm groaned. 'Can don't say that word, can or not?'

'Sorry! Sorry! I meant romance!'

Yi Ling groaned. 'Can don't say that word, can or not?'

I gulped. 'Err …'

'Joking lah!' She elbowed me in the ribs and everybody cracked up.

'Phew!' I drew the back of my hand dramatically across my brow. 'Wah! You really had me worried!'

'Cannot be so serious one lah! Come, drink some more.' She topped up my glass then raised hers and we clinked them together.

'It's too bad though. Sally was such a hardworking student — I took her for English last year.' John said. 'Her spoken English was horrible but her written was actually pretty good.'

'Well, she did read quite a lot,' I commented.

'How do you know that?' asked Sharm.

'She was a regular customer … at least she would come regularly. Rarely bought though.'

'Really? What did she like to read?'

'Donno.' I shrugged. 'Romance? No, no, please don't hit me!' I immediately raised a protective arm to shield myself from Yi Ling, getting a pretend blow from her and a laugh from John.

'Did anybody else teach her?'

Yi Wei pointed at himself. 'Geography.'

'I did too,' Yi Ling said. I looked at her in surprise. 'She was taking art as one of her subjects. She wasn't bad, actually,' she said reflectively. 'Her perspectives were quite good.'

'She was very quiet though,' Jeevan said. 'I had her for

Science last year and if she hadn't been sitting right in front, I'd never have known she was in the class.'

'You guys are making me feel like a bad teacher!' Sharm pouted. 'I didn't even know she was one of my students until I heard her name. I can't help it if I'm bad with faces!'

'Ooh ... bad teacher!' Jeevan wagged a finger at her.

'I'm not much better with faces.' I nudged her consolingly. 'I even saw her on Saturday night and didn't recognize her.' I grimaced. 'Auntie Fong was the one who identified her from the sketch in the newspaper.'

'You saw her on Saturday? Seriously?' John was surprised. 'Where?'

'Oh ya .... I was out with some friends and happened to see her,' I said vaguely, wondering if I shouldn't have mentioned it. Was this a secret? Inspector Rizwan hadn't said. Maybe I'd better not say so much.

'Really? You never said.' Sharm smacked my arm. 'How come you didn't say? Was it at Zouk?'

I should have known she'd want details. 'Wah, you almost finished your drink. Come, I'll fill your glass!' I picked up the almost empty jug and did so over her protests. 'Should we get another jug?'

In the ensuing debate for and against, I saw John smile knowingly as he mouthed 'smooth' at me. I shrugged a 'Who? Me?' back at him and he laughed.

Now that I was actually looking at him, I could see that he was good-looking enough that I was sure that a number of his students had a crush on him. Oval face just rescued from looking effeminate by a strong jaw. Thick wavy hair. Soft brown eyes that reminded me of caramel were fringed with thick eyelashes. Was that a mole beside his eye?

I wondered if Sally had had a crush on him. I couldn't remember who I'd had a crush on at her age.

Aged 10, it was Shanti's big brother who had come to our rescue more than once. Big and strong with an astonishing smile, he was our knight in shining armour; despite having a tendency to scold us thoroughly afterwards.

At 15, might it have been one of Beng's friends? Most of my teachers had been too old to inspire any interest. Or did they just seem old because I was younger?

Suddenly I felt a sharp elbow in my side. From Yi Ling. Jerked back to the real world, I hurriedly turned to her.

'Sorry! I missed what you were saying.'

'You've been staring at him so long, he's starting to blush.' I turned back to John and he really was blushing. A delicate pink tint that went all the way to the tippy tips of his ears.

'So sorry! I was thinking about something. I wasn't really staring at you.'

'I'm so jealous,' said Jeevan. 'John always gets all the attention.'

'I really wasn't staring at him!' But I faltered at his sceptical look. 'Well … not all the time, anyway. I was thinking about something and he was in my line of sight.'

More of the sceptical look.

'Really! I was just thinking and if you had been sitting across from me, I would have seemed to be staring at you instead.'

'I'm devastated!' John clutched at his chest. 'You have struck me to the core, you heartless woman!'

'So drama one.' Yi Ling rolled her eyes. 'Eh, this one not Drama Centre, you know? Can talk like a normal person, can or not?'

'So, what were you thinking about so hard?' asked Jeevan leaning forward and looking intently at me as though he was thinking of whipping out his magnifying glass to take a closer look.

I looked around and it seemed like everyone wanted to know. So many pairs of eyes on me; too much attention for my liking.

'Errmm ... I was wondering if any of his students had a crush on him.'

Everybody burst out laughing, except Jeevan who flopped back in his chair and let his head hang.

'I knew it!' he said resignedly. 'Pretty boy strikes again.'

'Hey! Who are you calling a "pretty boy"?'

'Children, children, play nice otherwise no dessert for you,' chided Sharm.

'How are you going to stop them from ordering dessert?' Yi Wei asked.

'Ooh ... is it time for dessert?' Jeevan perked up.

If being a teacher meant spending more time with people like this, maybe it might not be so bad after all.

8 Mar | Saturday

'Wah, it's hot like anything today,' I complained as I unlocked the shutters on the shop. Auntie Fong stood by and fanned herself with a newspaper from the small stack outside the door. The air was still and stale after the night. The air-conditioning system was still grumbling as it started up. So far, no cold air was being sent through the ducts.

I was functional but I wouldn't describe myself as happy. Bright light and loud noises made me flinch. Talking took effort. I was definitely on the cranky side.

'So how last night?' Auntie Fong asked as I started moving the shelves out.

'Fun. They're all quite playful.' I thought about the night before. 'And they drink a lot.'

'So, you got talk to the leng zai or not?'

'I talked to all of them. They're all —' But Auntie Fong had only one of them on her mind.

'So that leng zai, you think he's chup or not?'

'Which one ah?'

'The tall one lah! Sound like ang moh.' Oh, she meant John.

'Umm ... maybe? Or maybe he just studied in the US.'

'Married or not?' Oh no ... she's back on that.

'I don't think any of them were married.'

'All the married ones have to go straight home to their families.' The amused voice made me turn to see Jeevan standing behind me. Did he hear what Auntie Fong said?

He was wearing a short-sleeved shirt over faded jeans and didn't look at all like he had been drinking last night. He looked different somehow. Ah ... freshly shaved.

'Hi, what are you doing here?'

'To look at books, of course! This is a bookshop, right?'

Oops!

'Ya, but I didn't expect you to be here this morning. Especially after last night.'

'Look who's talking.' His eyebrow quirked quizzically.

'I didn't drink quite as much as you did.' He'd even had a couple of beers on top of all those margaritas.

'Ah ... but I've had a lot of practice.'

'Anyway,' I reverted to bookshop assistant. 'Are you looking for anything in particular?'

He shrugged. 'I'll just browse for now,' he said and proceeded to do so. I left him to it as I did my morning chores.

Auntie Fong left for her coffee break, leaving just me and Jeevan in the shop. Matt opened up and soon started blasting his favourite morning selection 'Everybody wants to rule the world'. I guess my hangover was easing because I didn't feel the urge to murder him.

'Well, that's a cheerful start to the day,' Jeevan commented as he came up to me. He was holding a John le Carré, *Tinker Tailor Soldier Spy*, I noted approvingly.

I laughed. 'That's his view of how the world works. Don't worry. He'll get happier after this. Find anything interesting?'

'Mmm … I was wondering if you ever came across *The Silver Pigs* by Lindsey Davis.'

'Ooh … that's a good one. I haven't seen any of that series in a while though,' I considered. Certain customers like to build their series and I suspected that's what happened to our copies of the Falco series. 'You might want to try another bookshop.'

'It's okay,' he sighed.

'Have you tried Steven Saylor's Gordianus the Finder?' I pulled *Roman Blood* out for him. 'Another Roman detective, but much earlier. Before Caesar, I think.'

He studied the blurb, flicked through a few pages.

'Worth a try,' I urged.

'All right.' He snapped the book shut and handed both to me. 'I'll take it.'

'Great! That'll be twenty-four dollars.' I rang up the two books and stamped the date on the slip pasted on the flyleaf. 'If you return them within three weeks, you'll get $19.50 back.'

'Okay.' He examined the date stamp. 'Due on the 30th. Shouldn't it be the 29th?'

I gave him a horrified look, went back to the calendar and counted again. He was right. I took the books back, scratched out '30' and wrote '29' above each date stamp before handing them back to him and picking up the date stamp to correct it as well.

'Sorry, I can't count to save my life.'

He chuckled. 'Sharm told me at the bus stop that you'll be starting at NIE soon.'

'Ya …' I sighed.

'Don't worry so much yet. NIE is a breeze. Just wait until

you're actually teaching. Not only do you have to teach, you have to do admin and then you have deal with the parents.' He shuddered.

'Are the parents so bad?' He was definitely not selling me on a career in teaching.

'Frankly, the students are comparatively easy. Granted you have problem cases but the parents …'

He considered then corrected himself.

'Some parents. Most of them are okay but the ones that aren't, they're really demanding. "My daughter this", "my son that" and then you have Mr Song — Sally's father. He's really something else. Do you know he actually contacted the school to ask us when we were going to send him the pek kim. Can you imagine?'

'Send him the pek kim? Isn't he going to hold a wake?' I had the vague impression that you didn't have pek kim without a wake.

'Donno lah. It just feels wrong. I never met him when I was teaching Sally, you know, only her mother.'

'What was she like? The mother, I mean.'

He pondered then shook his head. 'Not terribly memorable. Nice enough, I suppose.'

Auntie Fong returned carrying an iced kopi and Styrofoam box of chicken rice.

'Anyway, got to go. See you around,' he said as he left, books in hand.

'Wah!' Auntie Fong said. 'Just met you last night and he's already back here.'

'Nothing to do with me. He was looking for books.'

'Who shows up to look at books at opening time on a Saturday after a night out drinking?' Auntie Fong rolled her eyes exasperatedly. 'He came to see you.'

'No lah!' I wasn't in the mood for this.

'So stubborn,' she sighed but let it drop, picking up her newspaper and immersing herself in it.

I finished cleaning and gave the counter a final wipe before heading to the toilet to wash my hands. As I dried my hands, I looked in the mirror. The closest description would probably be 'average'. Average eyes, average nose, average mouth, pointy chin. And way too short. I ran my fingers through my hair and left.

Back at the shop I picked up The Bag and said goodbye to Auntie Fong. She just grunted.

I only waved in passing to Matt who was rearranging his CDs as I left. I wasn't in the mood to chat.

The sun outside was too bright and too hot. I dithered for a while then took the bus home. I felt unsettled. I felt like an overwound clock. I wanted to do something. I just …

When I got home, Ma told me to keep an eye on the clothes she had drying on the poles then left for her mahjong game. I nodded then got my shorts and towel and went to have a cold shower. While I was in there, I worked off some of my excess energy cleaning the bathroom walls and floor. It had been a while and the accumulation of soap scum was starting to bug Ling to the extent that she was bugging me about it every night.

I felt better after that. Wrinkly as a prune with the multiple showers but clearer about what was bothering me. Mr Song.

I opened the folder and pulled out Sally's photo. And after

that the copy of her letter. I rubbed my eyes and nose.

If Mr Song is asking people to give pek kim, surely he would talk to me if I showed up to give him some ... But the problem was that I didn't know where he lived.

The brightness of the day had disappeared while I sat at my table. Dark clouds filled the sky. I headed to the kitchen window and started bringing in the bamboo poles laden with laundry. I had just brought in the last one when a bolt of lightning split the sky followed almost immediately by a crack of thunder made me jump. Fat drops of rain started falling and soon it was sheeting down.

I reached my hand out into the rain. Each drop hit so hard it hurt.

* * *

We sat around the table tucking into our dinners. After a break, the rain had come back just as I left home and now a storm was rampaging over us. Most people had moved to the enclosure formed by the stalls.

Ours was a table on the outside. Although the rain beat down on the roof and you could still hear the chatter coming from the inside, it was still quieter. At least we could hear each other talk. Still sheltered but I could feel the slight mist from droplets of rain hitting the ground. Combined with the wind that blew around us, it cooled the air so that it felt almost like air-conditioning.

I tucked into my beehoon goreng putih (always good, topped with salty, crunchy fried ikan bilis) but was really coveting the tulang that Yong was savouring. I sniffed the sweet, spicy, meaty aroma that wafted up from the dish of red stew wistfully.

'That's really bad for you, you know.'

'What? The tulang?' Yong asked. 'But it's sooo good!' He picked up a bone and sucked it loudly.

'High in sodium, fat —'

'You want some, is it?'

'Yes please!!!!' I stood up, reached over and my spoon dived into his bowl and came away full of the rich sauce. I dumped it on my beehoon before licking the spoon. 'Ooh … yum!'

'And now I have your saliva in my food,' Yong said glumly.

'It's okay, I'm not sick.'

Shanti laughed and stuck in her spoon as well. 'And now you have my saliva too.'

He shook his head at her but smiled. She smiled back. Their gazes locked for a long moment. I watched that small intimacy with interest. They've been going together for a while but I rarely saw any display of affection.

Finally they looked away from each other. Shanti realised I had been watching and frowned at me warningly. I wrinkled my nose at her.

Sharm poked at her soto ayam unappreciatively and sighed.

'What's wrong?' Nora asked her.

'Can't be still hungover, right?' I asked. 'You didn't drink that much.'

She groaned. 'Don't talk to me, you unnatural bitch. You're so perky, you're disgusting.'

'Oi! Who you calling "unnatural"? Normal people's hangovers just don't last so long. You want unnatural, look at your colleague, Jeevan.'

She lifted her head at that. 'Jeevan? Why?'

'He showed up at the shop just after we opened this morning, looking all bright and chirpy. He definitely didn't have a hangover.'

'What? He was there so early? Wah ...' Sharm marvelled. 'It's a miracle!'

'Huh? What you talking about?' Maggie pounced.

'He hates waking up early,' Sharm chortled. 'Every day he complains about it.'

'Not that early what — we opened at ten o'clock and he came at about ten-thirty.'

'Still ... for him to come out that early ...' Sharm smirked meaningfully.

'Ooh ... what does he look like?' Maggie looked from me to her.

'Slim, black hair, glasses.'

'You know you just described Yong, right?'

I looked at Yong. He looked back at me solemnly, the end of a mutton bone in his mouth.

'Much darker, black-framed glasses and nicer hair.'

'Ooh ... nicer hair, is it?'

'Ha! I'm going to tell him you think his hair is nice!'

'No need!' I glared at her but Sharm just laughed.

'Although you seemed more interested in John, right? The way you were staring at him last night.'

'I wasn't staring at him! I was thinking ... and he just happened to be in front of me.'

'You made him blush!' My ears got hot as they all turned

amazed eyes on me.

'Good-looking, is it?' Nora asked.

Sharm fanned herself with her hand.

'Damn hot! Tall, slim, a bit boy band. All he has to do is smile and the admin staff can't do enough for him.'

'But Mei's not really the boy band type, is she?' Maggie said. 'She seems to prefer the talkative type.'

'Hmm ... She prefers them or they prefer her? People attach themselves to her all the time.'

'Eh, I'm right here, you know?'

'Ya,' Maggie agreed. 'Old, young ... Mei, remember that boy that got onto the bus — he squeezed past me to sit on your lap and tell you all about his new toy. His mother was so embarrassed but he wouldn't budge.'

'Half the time, they're taking advantage of her. Mei, remember that cleaner who asked you to look after her bag while she went to toilet.' Shanti shook her head.

'She had her lunch in it! And you know how people are about taking food into the toilet ...' I protested.

'The fact is that you just sat there and waited twenty minutes for her to come back.'

'Don't forget that crazy woman on the bus —'

'Enough! Enough!'

'And, of course, we mustn't forget Richard,' Nora added.

'Richard?' I asked surprised.

'You forgot already? He used to follow you around like a puppy.'

'No lah! He was chasing Maggie. I was just the shoulder he cried on.'

A particularly strong gust of wind spattered rain across our faces and, as one, we picked up our food and retreated to a table inside.

* * *

Chan Family Home

Teck Wai came home late that night to find his mother sewing up a tear in his shirt.

'Sek zor mei?'

He rubbed his face wearily then stretched. 'Hai yaa ... I was so busy writing reports, I didn't have time to eat.'

She shook her head. 'Always one. Go and bathe. I'll cook something.'

'So late already, no need lah.' He went to his room to drop his things and picked up a pair of shorts.

'How can don't eat? I'll cook some Maggi mee — very fast so quickly bathe!'

In the bathroom Teck Wai shed his clothes and dumped them in the laundry basket just outside the door before turning on the shower to full. The blast of cold water shocked him awake before the water heater started to warm it up. He quickly soaped and rinsed and was drying himself when the smell of cooking made his stomach growl.

By the time he opened the bathroom door, the bowl of hot eggy noodle soup with cabbage, fragrant with sesame oil and a dollop of fried chilli, sat on the table with chopsticks and spoon.

'Sek, sek!' his mother urged and sat down to watch him dig in.

'Anything interesting happen today?' he asked.

She laughed. 'Last night Mei's friend came and took her out with her teacher friends. Wah! They must have drunk a lot! This morning she looked like kiam chai.'

Teck Wai grunted. She eyed him consideringly then continued. 'But today both the men came back to see her. First thing in the morning already got one. Then after lunch got one more. Some more this one really leng zai! Tall, slim, fair, big eyes …' She sighed in satisfaction. 'If I was twenty years younger …'

'So old already still looking at men!'

'Still got eyes, okay?' She cut her eyes at him then chuckled. 'But he really no luck. By the time he showed up she chau liao. So maybe he'll come again tomorrow.'

Some chilli went down the wrong way and he started to cough.

'Ah Wai ah, can don't eat so fast, can or not?' she chided him smugly.

9 Mar | Sunday

It was another hot day. So hot, so humid ... the kind of day that you just want to find some place with aircon and never leave.

Even with air-conditioned buses, I was sweating and limp by the time I reached Holland Village.

When I got to the shop, Auntie Fong was already waiting for me looking smug.

'Hoi! Yesterday that leng zai came looking for you!'

'Leng zai?' At first, I didn't know what she was talking about, then light dawned. 'You mean John?'

'Err ... that teacher... you know lah!'

'What did he want?'

'To see you lor ...'

'What for?' I asked bewildered.

'What you think?' She clapped her hands impatiently. 'He's probably coming again today. Go! Go! Make yourself pretty!'

'Plastic surgery takes a long time, you know!'

'Hai ya! Just go!' She took me by the shoulders, turned me and pushed, not lightly either. I stumbled out of the shop.

In the toilet, I splashed water on my face then looked in the mirror. What a wreck. I splashed more water on my face and pushed my wet hands through my hair, trying to make it look more presentable. All I can say about my hair is that it's thick and healthy. Takes forever to dry so I keep it short. Saves time in the morning.

I splashed more water on my hair until it was damped down enough so that it at least looked neat. That was all I could do and no more. I squared my shoulders and went back to the shop.

Auntie Fong looked disapproving but resigned.

The Sunday crowd is late and comprises mainly families with children so I was kept busy keeping an eye on and helping kids reach for stuff while their parents also looked for books. It was a surprise when I looked up to see John smiling down at me.

'O-oh! Hi!' I stammered, surprised.

'Hi, Mei.' His faint American accent gave his words an exotic air. 'How are you doing today?'

'F-fine! Fine!' I took a breath to calm down. 'What are you looking for today?'

'I was going to browse a bit, but it looks like it's packed today,' he said looking into the shop.

'Sundays are like that,' I laughed. 'People run errands on Saturday and on Sunday they come out for fun.'

'Me too. But it looks like you're too busy.'

'I take my days off when there are fewer customers.'

'Oh … so what time do you get off today?'

'We close at 5.30 but we have to close up the shop —'

'Would you have dinner with me tonight then?' His sudden invitation took me by surprise.

'Sorry, but I already have something on.' He looked so crestfallen that I added, 'But it's not until 7.30 so we could have a coffee before I go … if you like.'

His face brightened. 'I'll come back at 5.30 pm then.'

'Six, please — we have to close up the shop. See you then,' and turned my attention to the little girl who was tugging at my shirt.

* * *

I was just pushing in the postcard stand when John showed up.

'Oh! You're early! Sorry but can you come back in —'

'Go! Go!' cried Auntie Fong. 'I can finish here!'

'I —'

She shoved The Bag into my arms. 'Go!'

I laughed and turned to him. 'Let's go!'

I thought we were going to go to the hawker centre or, if he was feeling hot, maybe to McDonald's. But he headed to the basement carpark instead. Following him, I studied his back. Broad shoulders, tapering to narrow hips, with thick wavy hair, a brown that was just a couple of shades lighter than black. I wondered if it was natural. If he coloured his hair, wouldn't it be lighter?

He led me to a silver sedan. It was a Toyota, which I knew because it is the only car logo I can recognise.

'Wow, you already have a car!' I said as I got in.

He laughed sheepishly. 'My mom makes me take her everywhere so I figured it would be easier if I had a car. So now she has a personal chauffeur.'

'So lucky! My mom has her own taxi driver — but he never wants to take her anywhere,' I chuckled.

He backed out of the parking lot, carefully with a lot of checking in all directions.

'So, your dad drives a taxi?'

'For over twenty-five years.'

Traffic was not as bad as I expected. I guess everybody went home to rest up for tomorrow. Soon we were driving up the ramp into the Liat Towers carpark.

'We're having coffee here?'

'We're going to Starbucks. Have you been there before?'

'Err … no.'

Now, I love my kopi gao siu tai. It's what starts me up in the morning, keeps me up after lunch and gives me that extra boost towards the end of the day. When Coffee Bean & Tea Leaf opened in Scotts Shopping Centre middle of last year, I went with the gang and nearly fainted when my coffee and cake came up to over $10. All very nice but frankly, for that same amount, I could have a full meal on Orchard Road and breakfast, lunch and dinner outside the CBD. Call me kiam siap but I have better things to waste money on.

So, when Starbucks had opened its first branch in Singapore last December, I hadn't really bothered to join the queue to get in.

This evening Starbucks was relatively quiet, meaning to say every table in the air-conditioned shop was occupied but most of the seats outside were empty. I looked at the menu, blanched at the prices then ordered a tall cappuccino. John ordered a double espresso and insisted on paying for both drinks.

We took our drinks outside. It was warm and humid but I could watch the people going to and fro over John's shoulder. Tourists mingled with locals, everybody heading somewhere. It felt strange to be just sitting and watching the world go by. I wondered if I would feel the same sitting on a sidewalk outside a bistro in Montmartre. Suddenly I realised that John was saying something.

'Sorry, could you repeat that?' I smiled apologetically. 'I'm afraid I was distracted by all the people going by.'

'I was just asking how your day was.'

'Oh, it was fine. Busy. How was yours?'

'Love Sundays. Being able to sleep in is great. And then not having anywhere to be ...'

I laughed. 'So, you weren't able to sleep in on Saturday?'

He made a face. 'No. I had to go to school for club activities.'

'Which club are you looking after?'

'ELDDS.'

'Fun?'

'Yeah but they are a handful! We took them to a matinee performance last month and I was so glad that Yi Ling and Jeevan agreed to come help. Two hundred kids in school grounds, you know they're not going to get lost. Same two hundred in the Drama Centre?' He rolled his eyes. 'It was like trying to herd cats!'

I laughed at the image of the three of them trying to control two hundred kittens in school uniform, all going in different directions.

'How long have you been teaching?'

'Oh, a couple of years. Let's see. I graduated in 1990 in the US, then I worked in advertising there for two, three years but I didn't really like it so I came back home in 1993? Applied to NIE and came out in ... '95. Almost two years.'

'So how does teaching compare to advertising?'

'Good question.' He pondered. 'They're so different, it's hard to compare.'

'I mean, when I was in school, it seemed like all we did was tests.'

'Yeah ... well, teaching here hasn't changed much since then.'

That didn't sound like much fun ... I'd been anything but exam-oriented and it seemed to be all teachers were interested in. I'd lost count of the number of notes I'd carried home by the time I was in Sec 2. I was just lucky I'd managed to get through the exams with minimal problem. The final exams anyway. Monthly tests and pop quizzes, not so good.

How was I going to survive the system from the other side? I sighed and realised that he was still talking.

'... but with all that, I do feel it's rewarding but you know, when something happens like with Sally, it really throws you for a loop.' He sighed sadly.

'Do you know if the police have made any progress?'

He shrugged. 'They keep coming by, asking questions, poking around and generally making a nuisance of themselves.'

'But they haven't said anything?'

He coughed a brief, unamused laugh. 'You must be kidding. They ask and ask and never say anything. Well, not to us teachers anyway. Maybe they update the principal.'

We lapsed into a brief silence then he checked his watch and asked, 'What time do you have to go?'

I checked the time on my own watch. I'd finished my coffee so I could actually leave now but he was still sipping.

'It takes about thirty mins to get to the restaurant so ... in about five minutes?'

'Hmm … why don't I take you there so you'll be less rushed?'

'Oh no —' I started but he broke in.

'It'll give me more time with you.' His eyes were very warm as he smiled at me.

I could feel the heat rise into my face. 'Uh … okay.'

He swigged the rest of his coffee and got up. 'Shall we go?'

As we walked to his car, he said 'Would you be free for dinner on Tuesday?'

'Sure, where?'

'I'm in the mood for a steak so I was thinking of Fosters.'

Hmm … that was somewhat on the steep side.

'Have you ever been to Colbar?'

'Colbar?'

'It's this little open-air place on Portsdown Road. They serve British-style food: steaks, grills, fish and chips. A lot of expats go there.'

He shrugged. 'Okay.'

We got into his car and he asked, 'Where to, madam?'

I repressed an eye roll and said, 'Jalan Bukit Merah, please. We're having dinner there.'

'So, who's the "we"?'

I laughed. 'My sister's getting married soon so we're meeting with the groom and his parents to discuss the wedding plans.'

'How soon?'

'Next month.'

'Kinda late, right?'

'Oh … it's mostly done; it's just the final details.'

'I see.'

'Can't wait, really,' I chuckled. 'Ling's being so fussy over the details, it's driving all of us crazy. Pity Alex — he's the groom.'

John laughed and shook his head. 'You only get married once.'

'Huh,' I sniffed. 'No excuse.'

'Wait until it's your turn!' he teased.

'So not going to happen.'

'What? You're not planning on getting married?'

I opened my mouth to say 'No!' but stopped. I don't have a specific objection to marriage or getting married per se. I just couldn't imagine me being married. Not so much a failure of imagination but I like my alone time and I rather thought that would be lacking in a marriage.

'Well, I'm not planning to go husband hunting any time soon.'

'I see.' Then, 'Where should I drop you?'

'Just here is okay.'

'I'll turn in and drop you.'

He turned in and made a circuit around the parking lot before he stopped.

'Shall I come get you from Can-Do at six o'clock?'

I paused in the act of getting out.

'I'm afraid we only close at 7 pm on weekdays so the earliest I can leave is 7.15. Why don't you all go ahead and I'll join you later?'

He gave me a funny look. 'It's just you and me, Mei. I'll come get you at 7.15.'

I went hot with embarrassment and mumbled 'Okay, bye' as I made a quick exit from the car.

* * *

Thanks to John, I was actually the first to arrive. I ordered tea and sat at the table, staring into space and digesting what had just happened. It's not like I haven't been on dates before, but they had always been with people I'd known a while. People who had gotten to know me. So, to be asked out of the blue by someone I'd only met once, and a pretty boy at that … I was surprised. Was I flattered? Or suspicious? Was I over-thinking this?

'Wah, Mei! You're so early!'

Alex's parents, Uncle Richard and Auntie Kim, had arrived. They sat down across from me. Uncle Richard used to have his own business. He sold it a few months ago and likes to joke that it was because he needed the money to pay for the wedding. He was looking relaxed and happy in a short-sleeved batik shirt. Auntie Kim looked surprisingly stressed. A sweet-faced lady who is an excellent cook (I know because they had us over for dinner before), her normally serene smile seemed a bit forced. Was it due to the wedding?

'Uncle Richard, Auntie Kim! Wah! You're looking good!'

'He he he! Retirement is the best!' he laughed. 'I get to stay home every day with my beautiful wife!' He turned and gave Auntie Kim a smacking kiss on the cheek.

She patted his arm smiling weakly. 'I think we haven't spent so much time together since we were on our honeymoon!'

'Richard! Bee Kim!' Ah Pa said in greeting as he and Ma came up to the table. He picked up the menu and started discussing with Uncle Richard what to order. Ma smiled and sat down next to Auntie Kim and, in no time, they had their heads together discussing how the wedding preparations were progressing.

Ling and Alex showed up just as the food arrived. Alex looks a lot like his dad, i.e. stocky and fair with curly hair cut so short that you only ever see the curl when he's overdue for a haircut. Ling is slim and olive-skinned with hair down to her shoulders. Her standard work outfit is a black pencil skirt and whatever top she happens to put her hand on that morning. This morning, it was a black voile shell with a muted grey pattern. If it wasn't for her happy smile, you'd think she was going to a funeral.

'Wah! So much food!' she exclaimed. The fathers had gone all out. Braised duck, cold moulting crab and a steamed fish were the stars but there were also plates of jellied pork, deep fried chicken skin stuffed with sotong paste as well as oyster omelette, and of course bowls of steaming rice to eat with the dishes. Auntie Kim had insisted on ordering two vegetable dishes even though Uncle Richard (no great lover of greens) had pouted.

'Aiyah, once in a while no need lah!' he complained when she put good-sized servings of spinach and stir-fried mixed vegetables on his side plate.

'What you think? You're still a young man, is it? What did the doctor say the last time you went for check-up?'

'My cholesterol is too high,' he recited in a long-suffering voice that told me that maybe this wasn't the first time they'd had this conversation.

'And?'

'My blood pressure is too high.'

'Can eat like this already good. A little bit of vegetable won't kill you!'

She shook his arm. 'I want you to live long long so you better take care ah?'

His big smile returned and he put his arm around her and squeezed. 'Who wouldn't want to live long long with a wife like this,' giving us a big wink.

Ah Pa and Ma smiled but Alex sighed and shook his head.

Talk moved on to the wedding plans as we ate.

'Mei, don't forget that you are in charge of the jie mei,' Ling reminded me. Like I would forget. This was going to be the most fun part of the traditional wedding. We, the jie mei, would prevent Alex from coming in to collect Ling until he acceded to our demands. Apart from the hongbao, he was going to have to do a number of things to prove his love. I had a list and I'd already recruited Cora and a couple of cousins to help me in ward off the 'gate-crashing'.

Alex eyed me rather anxiously, worried by my evil grin. 'Nothing too weird ha?' he pleaded.

'Don't worry …' I reassured him. 'You got a lot of xiong di, right?' A smart groom always comes with an entourage of groomsmen to brave the jie mei's challenges in his place.

He groaned.

'He he! She's going to make you suffer,' laughed his unsympathetic father. 'Wah! This brings back memories ah?'

He nudged Ah Pa, who laughed and shook his head.

'Last time in the kampong much more fun. We had people playing music, even got lion dance. Now, only can decorate the car. So boring.'

Ling rolled her eyes, pulled out her wedding folder and, out of that, the check list. Hurriedly I pulled out my notebook and pen. The time for chitchat was over.

* * *

'Hey Sharm, can do me a favour?'

'What?'

'Can you find out the name of Sally Song's father for me? And maybe some contact details — phone number or home address.'

'What for?' And then she groaned. 'Don't tell me you're going to go and kaypoh.'

'No, no ... I just want to give my condolences and some pek kim.'

'Aargh! You ARE going to go and kaypoh!' Let's just say that Sharm knows me a bit too well.

'Okay, okay! I'm going to kaypoh. Just ask ask a bit, no harm, right? What's the worst that could happen?'

'What if he gets mad?'

'Then I say sorry and cabut lo ...'

There was a silence and, I swear, I could hear her eyes rolling.

'What if he gets mad and beats you up?'

'Err ...'

'See?'

'So, you think I should bring somebody with me?'

'I think you shouldn't go at all! It's a really dumb idea!'

I sighed. She was right and I couldn't think of any good arguments.

'Thanks, anyway, Sharm. G'night.'

'Forget about going to see Sally's father, Mei. Be smart.'

She hung up.

I put down the phone receiver and leaned back. Not enough. I swung my feet up on the sofa and drummed my heels. Who else could I ask? What was a good reason for asking?

10 Mar | Monday

'So how last night?' asked Auntie Fong. That was the first thing she said to me when I showed up. She was positively panting for details.

'Like that lor.'

'You ah, like trying to pull teeth. Don't shy shy leh! Where'd you go?'

'He took me to Starbucks.'

'Wah!!! So atas one! Nice or not?'

'Nice lah but so expensive! Go once or twice already pok kai.'

'So, what about him? Nice or not?'

'Nice!' I laughed. 'But must be rich. Already got car, and then he insisted on buying the coffee. $6 for one cappuccino!'

'Cap- cappu-? Kong si mi?' she asked, puzzled, then brightened. 'Wah, teacher already so rich one?'

'Donno lah. Teacher pay not that high. Maybe rich family.'

We pondered that for a while. Then she said, 'So how? Are you going out again?'

'Ya —' was all I got out.

'When ah?' she asked excitedly.

'Tomorrow night.'

'Going where?'

'Colbar.'

'Colbar? That old place? Why?'

'Fun what ... got atmosphere.' She gave me a stern look. 'Also not so expensive.'

'Gir', don't be so kiam siap, can or not? If you think you like him, and he likes you, must try.' she said sternly. 'Otherwise how to find husband?'

'Who said I wanted a husband?'

'If not, how? Live with your parents for the rest of your life, is it?'

'I could buy my own place ...'

'Buy a condo, is it?' She shook her head dubiously.

'I thought 35 years old single person can buy HDB?'

'Then who look after you when you get old? Mei ah, you got to think — next time, if no children, who's going to look after you?' She sighed. 'No need to talk about when you're old. When all your friends get married, have children then how? They won't have time for you like now.'

I opened my mouth then closed it again. What was there to say?

* * *

Auntie Fong was on her coffee break and I was dusting the books when I heard the phone ringing. I rushed over to answer it.

'Can-Do Bookshop, Mei speaking.'

'Mei, I'm glad you picked up! This is Jeevan here.'

'Jeevan? Hi, what's up?'

'I was wondering if you were free for dinner tonight.'

Seriously, what's going on? I've never been this popular. But he made me laugh so why not?

'Sure. Where to meet?'

'What do you want to eat?'

'Umm … something light. We went out for dinner last night and I ate too much.'

I heard a stifled laugh and smiled.

'Do you mind eating at a hawker centre? What I really want is fish soup.'

'Hawker centre is fine. Which one?'

'Ghim Moh?'

'Sure. What time and where to meet?'

'Roadside outside the market at … 7.30 pm?'

'Okay, see you then.'

I hung up bemused. Then picked up the receiver again to call Ma to tell her I wasn't having dinner tonight.

Auntie Fong returned while I was on the phone.

'Wah! Going out for dinner with the leng zai, is it'

'No lah! I'm having dinner with a friend.'

'Which frien'?' she persisted. I sighed and gave in.

'Jeevan.'

'Oh … the Indian one, is it? See? You just need to try a bit, already got fish.'

* * *

I managed to catch Lakshmi at her parents' shop after school. It looked like she had just come from school.

'Hi, Mei! How's things?' she asked cheerfully.

'Hey Lakshmi, any idea how I can find out Sally's father's name?' I'd been thinking of how to do this all day and was in no mood for small talk.

She looked at me in surprise.

'Huh? Why?'

'I'm wondering whether they've released Sally's body for the funeral.'

'Hmm …' she pondered, head cocked to one side, just like a bird. 'My mother might know.'

'Your mother?'

'She was on the PTA committee and since they would send letters out to parents, she has a mailing list. Wait, let me ask.' She turned and went into the shop calling 'Ma!'

I followed her in but stood back as Lakshmi did the talking. Auntie Ratna pushed up her glasses and turned to her computer. She opened a file and scrolled down and down. Then she hit Control-F and typed 'Song' in the Find box. She shook her head and scrolled down again.

'No result. Mei, are you sure it's Song, not Soong? We have a Soong here.'

Lakshmi shook her curls. 'Definitely Song. Sorry Mei, don't have.'

'Thanks, Auntie Ratna! But can you please try one more name? Mary Wong.'

I held my breath as she typed the name in the Find box and hit return and …

Yes! A result popped up: Mary Wong and an address.

'Wow, thanks!' She leaned back and I leaned in to take down the address.

'When you go to the wake, please give them my condolences as well,' she sighed. 'So sad to lose your daughter so young. Children should never die before their parents.'

'Ya, my mom says the same thing.'

'You put so much into your children that if they die, it must feel like a part of you died with them.'

She looked up at Lakshmi as she leaned on the back of her mother's chair. I could practically read her thought.

'That could have been my daughter.'

* * *

Jeevan was already standing where we'd agreed when I got there. After we found an empty table, he sat down and insisted I go get my fish soup first since I already knew what I wanted. Happily, the queue was not so long and I was soon back with my tray and he took his turn to get his food.

He came back after some time with a plate of duck rice. I was already eating; fish soup is much better eaten hot. I had gotten the version with lots of thinly sliced bitter gourd. The bitterness made the soup even more refreshing, washing away the memory of richness from the night before.

'Last plate, can you believe it?'

'Wah! So lucky.'

'How's the fish soup?'

'Just what I wanted. Hot, soupy and light!'

'What did you eat last night that was so rich?'

'We had dinner with my sister's in-laws-to-be and on top of all the dishes we ordered, we had orh-nee for dessert. Have you had it before? It's yam paste with ginkgo nuts. They cook it with lard … You usually only eat about a clay spoonful because it's that rich.' I sighed. 'Unfortunately since I was the youngest there, they made me finish what was left in the serving bowl. Cannot waste, right?'

Jeevan laughed. 'How much did you end up eating?'

I pointed at his bowl of soup. 'About that much. Talk about indigestion.'

'Oh, by the way, I've nearly finished *Roman Blood*! It's pretty good, thanks!'

'I thought you'd like it!' I said, pleased. 'Do you want me to put aside the next one in the series for you? I think it's still in.'

'That would be great! I'll come in later in the week.'

'So … do you spend your free time reading?'

'Oh, no. I mainly read on the way to and from work. Not much else you can do on the bus.'

'Me too. These days, it seems like it's the only time I get to read.'

'Murder mysteries,' he said unexpectedly. 'Why do you like reading murder mysteries?'

'Hmm … I didn't always have a penchant for mysteries. It's only after I read *The Murder of Roger Aykroyd* that I started to actively look for and read murder mysteries. When I finished her mysteries, I worked my way through Sherlock Holmes, then Father Brown and so on.'

'So, what is it about murder mysteries that makes them so addictive for you?'

'That's an interesting way of putting it. It's a good question.' I put my elbows on the table, pushing the tray aside. 'I think it's because there is always resolution … at least the ones I like have resolution. The mystery is solved, the murderer is caught.' I made a face. 'I wonder what that says about me. Probably that I'm an escapist.'

'Join the club.' Jeevan held his hand out and we shook hands.

'Sometimes life just sucks and it seems to be never-ending. I can see how it helps to have a good ending once in a while, even if it's only fiction.' He sighed. 'Like Sally's death. It seems to be going on and on. Even if you try to act normally, it's always there, you know?'

'Are you all looking at each other wondering if one of you did it? That's what happens in books.'

He shrugged. 'She was killed somewhere else so it could have been anyone. All I know is that it wasn't me.' He checked his watch. 'What do you want to do now?'

I checked my own watch. It was just past eight.

'Actually there's nothing much to do here but eat …' I racked my brain for some other activity.

'Unless you'd like to go for a walk by the river?' He eyed The Bag dubiously. 'If your bag's not too heavy.'

'Walk by a river? There's a river near here?' My eyebrows rose.

'Yup. It's very near.'

'Well … I don't mind checking it out. I've never been.'

We walked through the HDB blocks towards Commonwealth Avenue West. I thought we would be taking the bus but, to my surprise, he turned right to take a small path that led to a staircase down to the big drain that ran beside the road.

'You're kidding! That's just a drain, right?' I hung back.

'Come on!' he urged and, taking my hand, he pulled me along with him.

'This is actually Sungei Ulu Pandan,' he said waving his hand at the concrete-lined drain. I gaped at him in disbelief.

'It is! The Government lined it with concrete in 1978.'

'But why?'

'I'm not going to bore you with the details but you know that Bukit Timah Road used to flood all the time, right?'

'Ya?' Ah Pa used to tell us stories of those floods. They happened whenever there was a heavy downpour and the only way to get through was by boat.

'Well, they built tunnels to connect Bukit Timah Canal with Ulu Pandan River so that the flood waters would drain into the river. And then since there was a lot of development here, they had to widen the riverbed and line it with concrete to cope.'

'How'd you know all that?'

'I brought the Science Club down here to do an eco-study. You know, take water samples to check if it was suitable for sustaining life, etc.' He grinned. 'They did a good job of the report. They even went to the National Library to get the historical details, which is why I can now impress you with my vast knowledge.'

'So is the water able to sustain life?' I asked, looking down into the drain.

'Afraid not. Too much pollution and not enough oxygen.'

Well, that was depressing.

As we walked, the landscape, lit by the occasional streetlamp, changed from busy urban to a quiet tranquil countryside with just the buzzing chorus of cicadas and the thumping feet of an infrequent jogger. If you didn't look up to see the brightly lit tower blocks over the tops of trees, you wouldn't know you were still in Singapore.

I stopped and Jeevan stopped too.

'I can't hear any cars,' I said in hushed tones.

He just nodded and we continued along, enjoying the quiet.

That was only a short stretch though, and soon we were walking past the backyards of houses on the other side of the river, brightly lit and full of the noises that people make.

We crossed the bridge and climbed the stairs back up to the roadside and crossed the road to the bus stop.

'Where do you live?'

'Queenstown.'

'Aren't you on the wrong side of the road?'

'No problem. I'll cross back when you get on the bus.'

'Oh ... thanks.' He smiled as he held my gaze. I looked away, over his shoulder to check for any oncoming buses, suddenly overly conscious of myself. 'So, I'll hold *Arms of Nemesis* for you. When will you be coming to get it?'

'How about Saturday?'

'Morning okay, afternoon cannot.'

'You're busy in the afternoon? What about in the evening?'

I thought about it. 'Nothing on, why?'

'SSO is holding one of their concerts in the Botanic Gardens. I thought you might be interested.'

'Ooh, I've never been. What time is it?'

'Starts at six but it's good to be there earlier so we can chope a good spot. So, if you can be there by five-thirty?'

'Five-thirty? Can! Meet where?'

'How about the entrance gate at Napier Road, near Gleneagles?'

'Set — Oh, that's my bus coming! Thanks for waiting with me! And for showing me the river. Bye!'

'See you on Saturday.'

As I put my farecard in the machine, I saw him still watching me and waved. He waved back.

* * *

When I finally got home, I took the Residential Listings from under the phone into the bedroom. That got a comment from Ma, given the last time anybody had looked into a residential directory was, despite Ah Pa's dutiful annual collection of all the new directories, Residential, Business and even the Yellow Pages, before I was born.

I ignored them all and went into my bedroom, switched on the light and dumped the directory on the table. Wah, the print was so small! I even had to switch on the desk lamp as well. I flipped through the thin newsprint pages until I got to 'Sol-Son' then I had to go down the columns to compare each Song address with the one I had.

'What are you doing?' Ling asked, leaning over my shoulder.

'Nothing.'

'What? You think I'm blind, is it? What are you looking for?'

'Somebody's phone number.'

'Wah, like pulling teeth. Fine, be like that.' She sniffed and left.

I continued down the rows, name by name using a ruler so as not to lose my place. Who knew there were so many people named Song in Singapore!

I was about to give up hope then there the address was. Under the name Song Wing Hock. And, yes, there was a phone number.

11 Mar | Tuesday

With its colonial-style apartments, where NUS housed its researchers, surrounded by secondary forest, Portsdown Road was, I imagined, not much changed from the days of British rule.

John parked his car along Jalan Hang Jebat, a small dead-end road that branched off from Portsdown Road and led to Masjid Hang Jebat. On Fridays the road was always jammed with mosque-goers but this being a Tuesday we had no trouble parking right in front of Colbar.

John looked around as we waited to order at the counter.

'I didn't even know this place was here!' he exclaimed. When I looked surprised, he shrugged and said, 'East Coast kid.'

The old, rundown café is a favourite of expats looking to get away from what I once heard an ang moh wife term as 'the eternal sterility of Singapore'. I think its dilapidated condition actually attracted them, providing 'ambience' and 'character'.

Mismatched tables and chairs provided indoor seating and for some mysterious reason, an old-fashioned weighing scale stood at the door.

Two big refrigerators against the wall held bottles of soft drinks, imported beer and cider. Next to the counter stood a bookcase with big bottles holding sweets and snacks on top. In front of the counter was a Walls ice cream chest freezer.

We stood at the counter and studied a battered, laminated copy of the menu.

Finally, I opted for sausages, eggs, chips and peas — no steak for me after all. John ordered a sirloin steak with chips and beans. No fancy sauces, only a choice of sides.

After we ordered and paid (after a brief struggle over paying, which John won by unfair means, i.e. longer arms) I took our number and led John through the side door, past a couple of chunky long tables and out to the open-air eating area, where more mismatched tables and chairs were scattered. Most of them were occupied by people relaxing after the workday with a bottle of beer.

We managed to snag a wobbly table close to the outside and begged a couple of unoccupied chairs from the nearby tables.

'This was originally a canteen for the British Army,' I said as I tore a piece of paper from the back of my notebook. 'I thought it was spelled C-O-A-L until I actually came here and found out it was short for "colonial".'

'What's that?' John nudged my notebook.

'That? Nothing. I just like having somewhere to write random stuff.' I stuck it back in The Bag and bent double to stick the folded paper under a table leg. 'Can shake the table?'

John obliged and I pulled out the paper wad, refolded and replaced it then sat up.

'Ah … so much better,' I said, testing for wobble.

'What kind of random stuff?'

'Huh? You know … wedding stuff, errands for my mom. I have a mind like a sieve. In one ear, out the other.' I shook my head. 'My poor mother! If she asks me to buy something, I either come back with the wrong thing or with nothing at all.'

'It's surprising she hasn't given up all together.'

'No choice. My dad is driving all day so he's never near a phone and Ling usually works late so she rarely leaves work in time to buy whatever my mom forgot to get for dinner. I, on the other hand, am just a page away.'

'Maybe your dad should get a handphone.'

I laughed so hard, I nearly cried. 'What? Spend all that money so my mother can ask him to run errands?'

John smiled wryly. 'Not going to happen?'

'Die first. Ooh, food!' The young boy put two plates of food on the table, picked up the number and left. No forks or knives.

'I'll go get the cutlery,' John said and got up.

While he was gone, I stared out into the night. Too dark to see anything but I knew there was only some scrub out there. I wondered if I should bring anyone with me to see Sally's father. I wondered if John would come with me. But he would be working so there's no way he could make it.

I missed Shanti and how it was in our school days. Regardless of what we got into, we knew the other was always there to jump into the tangle and lend a hand. Admittedly I probably got her into a lot more trouble than the other way around. Now that she had a real job, I shouldn't involve her either. What if she got into trouble?

Lost in my thoughts, I jumped when John came back with, not only cutlery, but two ice-cold Tigers and a glass.

'I couldn't resist!' he grinned.

'Should you really be drinking so much if you're driving?' I said dubiously.

'One beer's not a problem. The other one's for you.' He put the second bottle and the glass in front of me.

'I'm not really a beer person …' I hedged but he was having none of it.

'Please, Mei …' He leaned over and looked into my eyes. I leaned back a bit. Too close! 'I don't like to drink alone.'

'Oh, all right.'

'Great!' He smiled and tapped my nose with a finger.

I sighed and reached into The Bag for my wallet.

'I'll be right back.'

And I was, with a can of Sprite and a straw. I poured the glass half full of beer and topped it up with the soft drink and stirred it.

John looked a bit disgusted.

'What? You've never drunk shandy before, is it?' I laughed. 'I'm not really a beer person.'

'What a Philistine!' he grumbled. I chuckled and we started eating. The sausages were really good — not hot dogs but proper sausages, yum!

'So, what do you do in your free time?' he asked.

'Umm …' I hastily swallowed my mouthful. 'Read, hang out with my friends.'

'What do you normally do?'

I laughed. 'We usually eat. Our favourite activity.'

'But you also go to clubs? You went to Zouk that day, right?'

'Only very rarely. That was a special occasion; we were celebrating a birthday.'

'Yours?'

'Oh no. If it were mine, we'd probably be eating somewhere,' I laughed. 'I live to eat.'

'I'd never guess that looking at you.'

'My friend, Shanti, says that all the time. I think it's all the exercise I get working in a bookshop. You know, carrying the books back and forth, up and down …'

'I suppose so.'

After a couple more mouthfuls, he asked me what I'd been up to so I told him about walking along Sungai Ulu Pandan with Jeevan. He nodded as if interested, but I could tell he wasn't and soon he was telling me about himself.

Turns out his parents are well off and sent him to study law in the US, but he had switched to English after a year.

'Why'd you change?'

'Law is a pain and since I like to read … I was thinking of becoming a writer.' He laughed deprecatingly. 'Think I already told you that I was working in advertising for a while before coming back.'

He leaned back in his chair and took a slug of beer from the bottle. 'Ah, this hits a spot.'

'I've been accepted into NIE,' I confessed. 'Starting in July.'

'Really? That's great!'

'Ummm … yeah, well … anyway, I've never been to the US, what's it like, really?'

'Well, for one, the portion sizes are a lot bigger!'

I left the talking to him after that, only putting in an occasional 'Oh' and 'Ah'. He'd already finished his food so I focused on finishing mine while he talked about studying and working in the US of A.

His face lit up as he told me about his road trip from San Francisco to New Mexico with his friends, complete with sound effects and hand gestures bringing life to the story.

It sounded like a lot of fun but in a totally different world from mine, the kind I only ever saw on TV.

12 Mar | Wednesday

Auntie Fong was quiet this morning, not a single question about last night. I wasn't sure why but I was surprised and grateful.

The morning passed peacefully but when I was packing up to leave, she asked me if I had plans for the afternoon as she always does.

Since my phone call with Sharm, I'd been thinking that I should let somebody know where I was going. Not that I was expecting to get into trouble but still, you never know, right?

So I casually said, 'I'm going to give my condolences to Mr Song. I heard he's holding a wake for his daughter.' Okay, stretching the truth a bit.

Auntie Fong looked blank for a minute. 'Who?'

'Mr Song.'

Then it clicked for her and she frowned. 'What for?'

'I feel really bad about Sally …'

'So, you want to kaypoh, is it?'

What is it with all these people assuming that I'm going to kaypoh? Never mind that this time that was exactly what I was planning to do.

She shook her head. 'Tch tch tch! Never die before, is it?'

I slung The Bag on my shoulder and gave her as cheeky a grin as I could manage.

'Of course never die before. But just in case …' I flipped over an old date slip, wrote down Jimmy Song's name and address and passed it to her.

Her eyebrows shot up when she read it. She stuck it to the cash register muttering 'Siao char bor! Mm tzai si!' as I left.

* * *

I stood outside the door of the Song family flat. I knew that Mr Song was in as I had called earlier. But let's face it, I was nervous. In my head I could hear echoes of Sharm's voice saying 'What if he gets mad and beats you up?' I looked down the corridor then up. Signs of occupation in the plants, the battered couches and the laundry hanging on racks but there was nobody in sight, only a sleepy cat stretched out on the couch a few doors down. Unlike their neighbours, the space outside the Song flat was bare.

I really didn't have any business there but hey, I had the address and, as Auntie Rosnah would say, I was gatal.

In other words, I was looking for trouble … just a little bit.

I reached up and pressed the doorbell.

'Mr Song?' I smiled as winningly as I could when he opened the door. 'I called you earlier? I'm Tang Siew Mei.'

'Ah!' He unlocked the gate and the padlock. 'Come in, come in!' His tanned face was wreathed in smiles, showing his small and rather stained teeth. I slipped off my shoes and entered.

The living room looked like it had once been loved. The furniture that had been carefully chosen was now scuffed and in need of a good dusting. The coffee table showed a number of cigarette burns and an overflowing ash tray.

There was a woman already curled on the sofa. Although I would never have described her as young, in her blue dress with her fair skin, her shiny, long black hair and bright red lipstick, she was very attractive.

'Sit, sit! Let me get you a drink.'

'No need, no need, err, Mr Song —' I sat down on one of the chairs and settled The Bag in my lap.

'Call me Jimmy! We all fren fren, right?'

Mr Song sat himself down on the sofa, first carefully pulling at his too tight pants to give himself room, and put his arm around the woman's shoulders.

I had initially thought he looked rather young to be the father of a fifteen-year-old but a closer look showed me the fine lines around his eyes and mouth. His coloured hair was fashionably undercut à la Beckham and slicked smoothly off his forehead.

In his rather shiny shirt and tight pants, he didn't look much like a father in mourning for his murdered daughter.

'Uh okay, Jimmy. I just wanted to say that I am so sorry to hear about Sally and give the pek kim.' I handed him the white envelope which he accepted. Surreptitiously he felt it, trying to figure out how much was inside, rather like a little boy receiving a hong bao during Chinese New Year.

'Such a good girl! She was very hard working one.' He tried to look sad.

'I heard that she was even working part-time.'

'Ya, the coffee shop, the ka—' he cut himself off.

'She had more than one part-time job?' I asked, surprised. If the poor kid had to work more than one part-time job and still managed to keep up with her schoolwork, she was a much better student than I had been.

'No, no.'

The woman laughed.

'Ah, Mrs Song —' I started. I doubted she was Sally's mother but who knew? Maybe Sally's death had brought her back.

'Bù shì!' the woman stopped me in Mandarin. 'I'm not Mrs Song. Just call me Helen.'

'Ah okay, Helen. I was wondering why Sally was working so hard to earn money.'

'This useless buffalo,' she elbowed Jimmy. 'couldn't be bo—'

'Ah hahaha!' Jimmy interposed hurriedly. 'She was very ambitious! Always saving money.'

Helen snorted but held her peace.

'So where else was she working? It must have been hard for her to keep up with her studies.'

'My Sally was very smart! She didn't need to study.'

Really, this wasn't going anywhere. I mentally crossed my fingers and put my foot in it.

'I was told by one of her school friends that the reason Sally was having to work was because you weren't providing for her. Is that true?'

His face changed, 'Who told you that? It's not true!'

Helen had had enough and let loose a torrent of Mandarin. 'You lying SOB!' she snapped. 'You never gave her a cent. No pocket money or even money to buy food. Chinese New Year also never give hong bao. If you weren't staying here in the flat, I doubt you would even have bothered to pay the utilities bill.'

His face twisted in rage. 'Give her money for what? She's just like her mother, that whore! She can go sell her backside also! What I care?'

'This kind of useless father!' Helen sneered. 'Proper fathers get a job and take care of their children! Not strut around being the big man sponging on everyone who doesn't dodge fast enough!'

'What for? She had a roof over her head, she was making good money at Ah Seng's! So give her money for what? She's big already — time for her to pay for herself!'

'Erm … excuse me —'

'Don't you think that if she finished school, she might have made something of herself instead of being a karaoke hostess?'

'You shaddup! Who you think you are? My mudder, is it? Get out!' He grabbed us each by an arm, dragged us to the door and propelled us out of it with a shove then slammed the door behind us.

Helen and I picked ourselves up and dusted each other off as we checked ourselves for damage. Since I hadn't put The Bag down, it was safely on my shoulder but Helen banged on the door and yelled 'Bastard! Give me my bag or I'll call the police on you!'

The door opened and said bag was flung out. Jimmy banged the gate shut and locked it, shooting the padlock bar home viciously.

'I'm so sorry for causing so much trouble,' I said to Helen as we walked away.

'Enh! That bastard will come crawling back to me when he cools down,' she replied cheerfully. 'The question is if I will take him back.'

'Huh?'

'That useless fellow can't hold a job. If not for me, he also would be selling backside — down in Desker!' She laughed heartily. 'He's a stupid fellow but damn hot, right? That tight ass —'

'Helen, he said something about Sally working at Ah Seng's. Can you tell me who Ah Seng is and where I can find him?'

Helen stopped and looked at me. 'Why do you want to know?'

'I don't know really ... but how can a girl so young get into so much trouble that somebody kills her? I guess I want to know why ... and it seems like the police also hit a dead end. Nobody wants to tell them anything.'

She looked at me for a while, then sighed. 'Really looking for trouble. What? You also want to die, is it?'

'No, but if I can find out more about what Sally was doing, maybe —'

She cut me off and leaned forward confidentially.

'Look, Jimmy doesn't know but Sally only worked at Ah Seng's for a while. I got him to hire her but she was no good at it. You gotta be able to sweet talk the uncles to get good tips but she was ...' Helen pondered. 'Not shy ... but she wasn't entertaining, couldn't joke with the uncles and make them laugh. Maybe she was too young. Maybe they were too old.'

She shook her head sadly.

'Anyway, she was only working there for a couple of weeks then she quit. Told Ah Seng she found another job then said bye-bye.'

'When was this?'

'So long ago, how to remember? Last year ... last year ...'

She squinted up at the ceiling for a bit then looked at me and shook her head. 'Maybe Hungry Ghost?'

'Did anything happen when she was working there?'

Helen pursed her lips and thought for a bit. 'Well, there was that asshole who liked to target her, probably because she was so young. You know some men, the younger the better. But he's harmless — now he's chasing the new girl.' She shrugged. 'Not as young as Sally but her acting is very good.'

'What's his name?'

But she just shook her head.

I thanked her and gave her my pager number on a page I ripped out of my notebook — just in case she thought of something.

And then we went our separate ways.

* * *

Over dinner that night, I thanked Ah Pa and Ma for being my parents. You never think about how lucky you are to have responsible parents until you come across the other kind.

Ah Pa looked at me like he thought I was crazy but Ma gave me a sharp look.

'What happened?'

So I told them about my visit to Jimmy. Luckily, they were so appalled by Sally's plight they never thought to ask me how I knew her or why I was visiting him.

13 Mar | Thursday

Auntie Fong and I had closed up shop for the day and were walking out when we saw Lakshmi and Nik giggling over some photos. We were just reaching them when Uncle Nathan charged out and grabbed Lakshmi by the arm.

'You stay away from my daughter!' he yelled at Nik and hauled Lakshmi into his shop. So drama.

Surprisingly, Auntie Rosnah, just outside her shop, just watched with her arms and lips folded. Nik looked distressed.

'What happened?' I asked, surprised because Uncle Nathan is usually the mildest of men.

Nik sighed. 'We were studying last night and lost track of time.'

'Wah! So focused one ah?'

Nik laughed a little sheepishly. 'I had soccer training yesterday afternoon and I was so tired, I fell asleep.' He rolled his eyes. 'Lakshmi also. The uncle who was clearing tables woke us up at about 9 pm.'

'Nine not so bad what …'

'Except that Uncle Nathan and Auntie Ratna were frantic because Lakshmi didn't come home for dinner and they didn't know where she was.'

Auntie Rosnah, who had joined us, rolled her eyes. 'If she's my daughter, I would pukul you teruk-teruk. Aku betul-betul tak faham macam mana dua-dua pun boleh tidur sampai tak sedar dunia.'[1] She smacked him up the back of his head. Hmm … I guess she was more upset than I realised.

'But where were you?'

'We were in McDonald's … aircon …' Nik sighed. I shook my head sympathetically.

'Well, looks like you're on your own …'

Nik grimaced.

'What's the problem?'

'Lakshmi's been helping me study geography — we've been working on it together — too many products. I can't even remember half of them.'

He brightened suddenly. 'Mei, can you —'

I rolled my eyes. 'I hate Geography! Don't you have other classmates to study with?'

Auntie Fong smacked my arm. 'Hai yah! If can help, help lah!'

Auntie Rosnah clasped her hands together and looked at me pleadingly. Nik gave me puppy dog eyes.

I sighed. Really no choice.

* * *

'Wah, long long never see!' Beng gasped at the sight of Ling at the table. 'You not working tonight meh?'

---

[1] 'If she's my daughter, I would beat you so badly. I really don't understand how both of you can sleep so heavily that you're oblivious to the world.'

'MC,' she replied smugly. 'I'm sick.'

'I don't believe — you jiak zua!'

Ling rolled her eyes. 'You know how many nights I overtime or not? Every week got four, five nights. Then Saturday also sometimes have to go in.'

'Wah! So siong one ah?'

'Audit like that lor. Everybody want same time. Lucky today I free so better I "sick" now.'

'Like that also can one ha? Suka-suka!'

'Got fever okay? Don't play play.'

I put the plate of freshly fried ngoh hiang on the dining table. 'Wah!' Ling cooed, leaning forward and sniffing happily.

'Oi! Sick person don' breathe all over the food,' Beng chided her.

Ling sniffed haughtily and opened her mouth to retort. I ducked back into the kitchen. Better to stay out of it. Being the youngest, both of them would come down on me like a ton of bricks if I dared open my mouth.

I counted out the plates for us, with forks and spoons and set them down next to the rice cooker and placed the rice scoop on top. We would come in and help ourselves to the rice before sitting at the table. I took out chopsticks and rice bowls to be filled for the parents.

'Mei ah, come and take the soup out.' Ma was ladling duck and salted vegetables into a big bowl and finally topped it up with the fragrant broth.

'Mmmm …' I breathed appreciatively until I touched the bowl. 'Sst!' I sucked in my breath in shock at the burning heat and immediately stuck my fingers in my mouth. Ma really has asbestos hands.

'Siao char bor! You should use the pot holders! No. Wash your hands first.' She put the bowl of soup on the counter and turned back to the stove.

Meekly I did as instructed and, thus protected, bore the bowl out to join the other dishes on the table.

'Mèi mei aaa' wheedled my sister. 'Can bring a small bowl for me? Sick person cannot share food.' I rolled my eyes but obediently went in to fill a small bowl with duck and salted vegetables. 'And rice, please!' floated in behind me.

'Go call your father. He should have finished bathing by now.' Ma came out of the kitchen proudly bearing a steamed fish.

'Ah Pa.' I knocked on the door just as he opened it. 'Lai jiak.'

I went back to the kitchen, filled the parents' bowls with rice, tucked their chopsticks in one hand and took them out to set before Ah Pa and Ma.

Next trip, I brought out Ling's soup and rice. Beng and Cora filled their plates with rice and brought them to the table. And finally I got to sit down with my own plate, after sticking clay serving spoons in all the dishes.

'Ah Pa, jiak. Ma, jiak,' we chorused before we finally got to tuck in.

'Mei ah, you need to learn how to cook properly.' Ma reached with her chopsticks for a broccoli floret.

'Again?' Ling queried. 'The last time it was what ah? Fried eggs, was it?' She nudged me with her elbow and grinned.

'I was peeling prawns,' I said with some dignity. 'She threw me out because I managed to stab myself in the thumb with a prawn head and was bleeding all over them.'

'What???' Cora gasped.

'Those things are sharp!'

Beng shook his head. 'Must have been day-dreaming again.'

'If you can't cook, then your husband how?' Ma said sternly.

'Aiyah, nowadays nobody cooks one lah. Who got time?' Beng was saying when suddenly …

'Husband?' Ah Pa had just registered what Ma said. 'How come suddenly she got husband?'

'Who's got a husband?' Cora asked. 'I thought it was Ling who's getting married?'

Four pairs of eyes turned on me. Caught with a full mouth, I just shrugged, still chewing.

'What husband?' Ling finally asked Ma.

'That girl has been going out with some teacher,' Ma said. 'Ah Fong told me this morning.' I spluttered and started to choke. Ling banged me painfully on the back and I got up to go to the wash basin in the kitchen.

Wah! Auntie Fong really has a big mouth, I thought as I coughed up the bit of rice that had gone down the wrong way.

When I finally got back to the table, I found out that Ma had been expanding on the subject.

'Wah! Rich man's son some more! Ho seh!' laughed Beng.

'Why you never say?' asked Ling.

I rolled my eyes. 'We only met one week ago. How can be so fast? Wah! Auntie Fong can really sing song.'

'Then why you always go out?' Ma wanted to know.

'Aiyah! Only two times with him. I have other friends, you

know!'

I started when the pager in my pocket vibrated. I checked the display and stuck it back in my pocket.

'Who paged?'

'Nobody.'

'Ho, ho, ho! It's that teacher, right?' Ling chortled.

Ah Pa finally put a stop to the teasing with a grumpy 'Enough, enough!' and talk turned to Ling's upcoming wedding. The restaurant had been booked for the wedding dinner months ago but they still hadn't decided on the march in.

'Are you going to do the dry ice thing?' Cora asked.

'Damn leh chey, leh,' Beng commented.

'But looks so romantic, right? Like floating in on a cloud,' Cora argued.

'You nearly fell down! You couldn't see where you were going.'

I remembered that bit. I also remember the man creeping behind them with a bucketful of water and dry ice … and a fan. I'd had a hard time not falling off my chair laughing.

'How about only have the dry ice at the entrance?' Ling asked.

'No point, people cannot see,' Cora dismissed the idea. I rather liked it though, I could imagine Ling in her wedding gown on Alex's arm, coming in on a misty cloud as though they were walking out of a myth or legend.

Later when Beng and Cora had left, and I had finished washing up. I called John back.

'Want to go see *Star Wars*?' he asked. 'They're showing the special edition starting tomorrow.'

'Ooh, yes!' No thought required. I'd been in love with Luke since the first time I saw the movie on TV. Ling had come out of our bedroom and was watching me with a wicked grin.

'Where's it showing?' Now she was kneeling beside me with her ear pressed to the receiver. I waved her off, much like I would an annoying fly but with no effect.

'Shaw Towers, Prince. Nine o'clock show, okay?'

'Great! We can eat first.'

'Where to meet?'

'Shaw Towers entrance?'

'Why don't I meet you at the MRT control station? Then we can go eat wherever.'

'Okay.'

'See you tomorrow.'

'Bye.' I put down the receiver and turned to look at Ling.

'What?'

'You've been keeping things from me,' she said and grabbing me by the arm, hauled me to the bedroom.

Of course I struggled but in the end it was no fight. Ling always gets her way. Alex really doesn't know what he's getting into.

Once the door was closed, she leaned back against it, folded her arms and said, 'What have you been up to, Mèi mei? Come and tell Jiĕ jie!'

I rolled my eyes. This is what she does when she wants to pull rank. I haven't called her 'Jiĕ jie' in years, although she still calls me 'Mèi mei'. It's close enough to 'Mei' and I pick my fights.

'What do you want to know?'

'So, who's this teacher? How did you meet?'

I sighed. 'He's in the same school as my friend Sharm. You remember her, right?' She nodded. 'I met him when we all went out for dinner about last week.'

'Last week? Only last week?' Ling frowned. 'So why Auntie Fong so kan cheong?'

'Donno lah! It's not like only got one guy. Other than Sharm and me, there were four people at that dinner so got six people leh.'

'So how come she acts like only got one?' Ling gave me the eye. I shifted uncomfortably beneath it. 'Mèi mei ah, what have you been doing?'

'I didn't do anything!' The eye continued. I gave in. I always do in the end.

'We went out for coffee on Sunday and dinner on Tuesday. But I had dinner with a different teacher on Monday!'

'Also guy?' she asked.

'Ya, so you see? Nothing special.'

'Wah ...' Ling marvelled. 'Suddenly you so hot property one ah?'

'Aiyah, don't like that can or not? Fren fren only lah!'

'You sure or not? Sometimes you very blur one.'

I rolled my eyes. 'Eh, not even one week, you think what? They desperate, is it?'

'Maybe ...?'

I rolled my eyes. 'Ha! You know the one Auntie Fong told Ma about? She calls him the "leng zai". Got reason okay?'

Her eyebrows rose. 'Really? Got picture or not?'

'What you think? I so rich got digital camera, is it?'

'You should bring him home for dinner so I can see,' she

giggled.

'I tell Alex then you know.'

14 Mar | Friday

Yock Li was in the shop looking at books this afternoon. I was a little surprised as she didn't strike me as the reading kind but I always welcome a reader.

She browsed among the romances, wandered through the mysteries and ended up next to me as I was shelving books in non-fiction. True crime is a very popular genre and we have a lot of that.

'Hi!' I greeted her. 'What are you looking for today?'

'Just looking …' She perused the titles available, occasionally pulling out one or another to read the back cover blurb.

'Are you into true crime?'

'Not really.'

Standing beside her, I could only see her profile.

'How are you doing?'

Her finger paused then continued running down the stack.

'I'm okay.'

'That's good,' I said, but looking at the bruises under her eyes and the downward tilt of the corners of her mouth, I didn't think so.

On impulse, I put my hand on her arm. She looked at me in surprise and I looked into her eyes and added earnestly 'But if you feel you need to talk to someone, I'm willing to listen, okay?' She hesitated then nodded, looking back down.

I left her to browse in peace and continued shelving.

When she finally came to the counter, she'd actually found a book she wanted. I rang up her purchase, stamped the date slip then handed it to her together with a second book. She looked at it in surprise, then at me.

'It's a little young for you but I always read *Anne of Green Gables* when I'm feeling down. It makes me laugh and cry and then I feel better somehow. Even now,' I said with a small laugh. 'I know because I just read it again.'

She just stood there looking at me. I looked back wondering what she was thinking, then I realised what it must be.

'Don't worry!' I added hastily. 'It's on me. I hope it helps.'

Her eyes filled. She opened her mouth, closed it. Then, after a nod and muttered 'Thanks', she hastily left.

I watched her go then sighed, rang up another book and stuck a $5 bill in the cash register drawer.

* * *

After we closed up the shop for the day, I walked out with Auntie Fong.

'Eh? Mei, you're not going home, is it?' she asked as I walked with her towards Holland Drive instead of leaving her at the foot of the stairs to cross the road to take the bus home.

'Ya, I'm going to see show tonight.'

'Wah! Young people really got energy,' she laughed. 'Lau lang all cannot see night show. Sure fall asleep one.'

Then she nudged me. 'You going with that leng zai, is it?'

she asked slyly.

'Ya …' I pondered on the likely consequence if I chided her for telling my mom I had a boyfriend, then decided that I wasn't brave enough.

'So how? You and he got …' and to my horror, made a gesture that no one wants to see an old lady make.

'Auntie Fong!' I gasped and pushed her hands down. She laughed and pulled her hands out from under mine.

'Young people aaa … you all so scared this kind of thing. So how? Got kiss already ah?' she demanded.

'No lah! Only just know him one week — how can so fast?'

'Eh! How many times you went out already?'

I paused, taken aback, then counted. 'Only two times … if you count the coffee.'

'Then today is number three.' She tapped her chin, thinking. 'Okay lah. Maybe a bit fast. But what you think? Got future or not?'

'Donno lah. One week a bit fast, right?'

She sighed and shook her head. 'No future. Ah Wai's father, second time I already know.'

Suddenly she brightened. 'Maybe Ah Wai still got chance!'

I rubbed my forehead. I was starting to get a headache.

'Auntie ah, he's not interested in me.'

She pouted. 'That boy! Work, work, work only. If he got no lou po, how to get sai mun chai?'

We'd reached the crossing to Ghim Moh, to my relief. I crossed over with her then made my goodbyes and turned left towards the MRT station. Buona Vista MRT station stands beside Commonwealth Avenue West, big and covered with very,

very green tiles. I can remember when they first built the MRT stations, that Beng was laughing about all the new public toilets since all of them were tiled. Makes for easy cleaning, I guess.

The tunnel underpass beneath Commonwealth Avenue West always smells of pee despite the public toilets being mere metres away.

As I went up the escalator, my tummy growled. I was soo hungry. Niang dou fu never lasts with me. I stuck a hand in The Bag and pulled out my last Polo mint and stuck it in my mouth.

The plan was to eat before the show but I couldn't decide where; that's why I'd asked John to meet me at City Hall. There really wasn't much fun food in Shaw Towers … Maybe we could eat at Middle Road … I had Thai food on the brain but Golden Mile was kinda far …

The station was full of people passing through the gates in both directions. I picked a queue and wended my way to the gate.

I slipped my farecard in the gate slot, plucking the thin card from the other end as I passed through. It was almost time to change the card, the coating was wearing off, showing black tracks.

When I stepped off the escalator, a train pulled up but it was packed and I was left standing on the platform when it pulled away. Always like that. Oh well, the next one would be coming in a couple of minutes. I stayed where I was, exactly where the train doors would open when the next train came but behind the yellow line. With the platform so crowded, I didn't want to be too close to the edge.

As the sound of the train approached, I turned to face out

across the track, ready to get on the train. The crowd surged, everybody manoeuvring to be first onboard. I tried to brace but suddenly I felt a hard shove in my back, right between the shoulders. I tried to catch my balance, spreading my arms like I was about to take flight, but the heaving mass behind me didn't allow me the space I needed and I felt myself falling forward.

Everything seemed to happen in slow motion,
the helpless sensation of free fall,
the roar of the oncoming train,
my hands reaching out to catch something,
anything to hold on to.

Abruptly, time returned to normal. I was jerked back by a big hand grasping my collar, much as you would grab a dog.

'Dey! You okay or not?'

Stunned, I turned my head and looked up into the dark face of large man. He frowned down at me, his monobrow truly fearsome. If I didn't feel like every bone in my body had turned to tofu, I would have kissed him. His hand, still holding my collar, shook me a little.

'Dey!! You okay or not?' he repeated.

I pulled myself together and tried to smile. 'Ya, I'm okay. Thanks.'

He grunted and pushed me ahead of him into the crowded train, fending off all attempts to cut in ahead of us. All through the journey, I stood next to him, focusing on his sturdy warmth to keep from trembling, biting my lip to keep the tears at bay. When I thanked him again before I got off the train at City Hall he only grunted.

Without him, the cold darkness threatened to overcome me and the shakes got worse and worse, so much so that the moment I saw John waiting for me outside the control station, I burst into tears.

John, appalled, wrapped his arms around me and pulled me into the shelter of a pillar. It took a while for the tears to subside. When I finally stopped shaking, he let me go and handed me his handkerchief.

'Sorry, sorry,' I mumbled, scrubbing my eyes. I was about to blow my nose when I thought better of it, handed it back to him and fished about in The Bag until I found my packet of tissues. Pulling one out, I asked, 'What time is the movie starting? Do we have time for dinner?'

'We don't have to go to see the movie — you're obviously upset, maybe I should just take you home.'

'You already bought the tickets, right? Mustn't waste them. What time?'

He sighed and pulled out the tickets — 9 pm. What with my crying fit, it was already 8.30 pm. No way we could walk all the way to the Golden Mile Complex for dinner and get to the theatre in time.

'Let's just have hotdogs at the cinema — I'll buy, okay?' I took his hand and towed him towards the escalator.

The revamped *Star Wars* was great! The new CGI on the big screen added a punch that you just don't get watching it on a TV screen. The big theatre was packed with excited people — only to be expected; it was the first screening, it was a Friday night and *Star Wars* has always been a favourite.

But for all that, I was distracted. Near death experiences tend to do that to me. Could it have been an accident? Maybe a pushy auntie got too enthusiastic … but no, the placement of the hand flat on my back, I could still feel it. Maybe somebody standing behind me put his/her hand on my back and pushed me so that I'd fall on to the tracks in front of the oncoming train.

Had somebody tried to kill me?

My muffled gasp was covered by Chewbacca's howl as the Millennium Falcon went into hyperspace. But John must have felt me stiffen; he turned to me and I could see the concern on his face. I just smiled and pointed at the screen. He smiled back and took my hand. The warmth of his hand felt good and somehow took away the fright of almost dying.

After the movie, we went for supper at Golden Mile; the hotdogs ($$!) had been light and even though I had also gotten popcorn ($$$!!!) I was so hungry I could have turned cannibal in a heartbeat.

I had mellowed by the time I'd put away most of the pad kra pao I'd ordered. John had been as hungry as I was and focused on eating his pad thai.

'Ooof … I'm so full!' I finally sighed as I drained the last of the tom yum goong from my bowl.

'So, do you feel like telling me what happened? Not that I mind having women fling themselves into my arms, although I must say I would prefer it if they weren't also crying, but it doesn't really seem to be your normal behaviour.'

'It's not and I didn't — at least I didn't fling myself in your arms.' I rolled my eyes. 'I just had a bit of a shock on the way to City Hall.'

'God, it's like trying to pull teeth. What happened?'

'I nearly fell on to the MRT tracks at Buona Vista.'

'What?? By accident?'

'Donno. Probably? You know how people tend to shove when the train is coming.'

'What??? You should be more careful!'

'I'm always very careful!'

He studied me. 'I've only known you a very short time but I get the feeling that's not true.'

'Would I lie to you?'

'I don't know … would you?'

'He he he —' My laugh was cut short when I caught sight of my watch. 'Aiyo! One o'clock already! I'd better go, got work tomorrow!'

'Relax! I'll take you home.' John drank the rest of his soup then held his hand out to me. 'Let's go.'

Rather shyly, I put my hand in his. I don't really like holding hands. Since the other person is almost always much taller, I always feel like a small child being led by Mommy or Daddy. But hey, he was driving me home. If a little bit of hand holding made him happy … well, it wouldn't kill me.

15 Mar | Saturday

I was a bit wary on my way to work, checking over my shoulder every so often. Didn't see anything though. I guess the prickling in the back of my neck was just paranoia. I decided that the MRT incident last night must have just been an over-excited commuter shoving. I couldn't think of any reason why anyone would have a reason to kill me. I mean, Jimmy Song might have been upset with me but it really wasn't anything he would want to kill me for. It must have been an accident.

Moral of the story, don't be so kiasu, just stay far away from the edges of platforms.

Note taken, I tried to put it out of my head. Even so, I found myself revisiting the terror of feeling myself fall, extrapolating to the gruesome sight of myself squished by the train wheels ... or would I be smashed by the impact of the train crashing into me.

The bus screeched to a halt, jerking me out of my abstraction. Time to stop dwelling. I pulled my current book out of The Bag and was about to reimmerse myself when my pager buzzed.

* * *

'Hi, John! What's up?'

'Nothing, I just thought I'd call to see how you were doing.'

'I'm fine, just reached the shopping centre.'

'Great! If that's the case, want to go out for lunch?'

'Umm … no, afraid I have plans. How about another day?'

'Sunday?'

'Afraid I'm working.'

'Dinner?'

'Okay.'

'Pick you up at 7?'

'Set.'

I put down the receiver and handed twenty cents over to the uncle at the counter before starting up the escalator.

* * *

'Hi! Just a minute.' I bent over to pull *Arms of Nemesis* from my shelf below the counter and presented it to Jeevan with a flourish.

'Thanks!' He put *Roman Blood* on the counter before taking the other book from me.

'Will you be looking for other books?'

'No … I still have the other book.' He put *Arms* back on the counter and hitched up the messenger bag he had slung cross-body before reaching for his wallet in his back pocket. Previously, he'd been going around empty-handed, something you will never see a woman do. Do men just need less stuff than women?

'How come you're carrying a bag today?'

He made a face. 'I brought home a few papers to mark yesterday so I'm taking them back to school after this.'

'What are you doing today?'

'Enh. Club activities. By the way, you haven't forgotten about the concert tonight?'

'No, I'm looking forward to it. 5.30 pm at the Napier Road entrance.'

He smiled, 'See you then!'

* * *

'So, what are you doing this afternoon?' Auntie Fong asked as she watched me pack up.

'My mom wants to go buy things in Chinatown. Also, we have to go to try on the cheongsams for the wedding.'

'Wah, so nice to have a daughter to go shopping with you,' she said wistfully.

'Why don't you ask Teck Wai?' I asked, well aware that he would take his mother anywhere she wanted.

'Not the same lah! Shopping with a daughter is different. He always ask why I want to buy. No fun one!' she lamented. 'Some more now he's so busy, can't even take leave.'

'Really? Why so busy? Is it because of Sally?'

'Aiyah, policeman always busy one. Every night come home late … if he comes home,' she sighed, looking down. To be by herself most nights, she must be so lonely. Auntie Fong likes having people around, going out. I knew she had friends with whom she had outings occasionally. But nights …

I nudged her and she looked up.

'Eh, next week you want to go out to makan or not? After we close shop we can go to Geylang and eat.'

'What?' she snapped. 'Feeling sorry for me, is it?'

'No lah ... I want to eat frog porridge but nobody else likes.' Which was also true. I tried it once and really liked it but everybody else is like 'Eee!' and won't even try it. 'I really want the one with dried chilli ...'

'Frog porridge?' Her face lit up. 'Can! Can!'

'Set! Next Sunday can? After we close shop we can go straight.'

I left her rubbing her hands together excitedly.

* * *

Ma was waiting for me at Outram Park MRT, just outside the control station.

'Where do you want to eat?' I asked.

'Kreta Ayer.'

It was too hot to walk so we took the bus even though it was just a few stops to Chinatown Complex. I don't know why I even ask Ma where she wants to eat whenever we come to Chinatown, she always wants to come here.

As usual, the place was hopping with long queues everywhere. Today she wanted to eat kway chap so I left her at an empty table and went to join the queue. Despite its length, the queue moved rapidly and soon I was carrying two bowls of soupy, slippery rice sheets, a plate of meat, spare parts, tau kwa and a hard-boiled egg as well as little saucers of chilli sauce back to Ma. I even managed to squeeze in a small dish of mui choy on the tray. The soup spoons were in the bowls and I had the chopsticks in my hand.

Focused on not spilling, I was taken by surprise when I heard my name called from behind me. I turned to see Helen behind me. Dressed down in jeans and a flowery blouse, she was carrying a plate of economy rice.

'Ni hao!' I greeted her. 'Very crowded today!'

She laughed. 'Always like this.' She followed me as I headed to where Ma was sitting. The other seats at the table were still empty so Helen joined us, sitting next to me. I introduced them and it didn't take long for Ma to find out that Helen came from the same province (Huilai County?) as her family and, of course, that meant that they were practically related.

'What are you going to do after lunch?'

'Ah … I have to go to the tailor to try on my cheongsam. Mei's older sister, Siew Ling, is getting married.'

'So good! When?'

'April 10. The fortune teller said that's the best day for them.'

'So good one! Who is she marrying?'

'Her classmate from poly. They've been together a very long time already.'

'His parents how?'

'I think not so bad. Siew Ling eats with them quite often so I think when she moves in no problem.'

'That's good. Very important to get along with the in-laws if she's moving in.'

'Ya, when I married, my mother-in-law was very fussy, so quite difficult.'

'Mmm, I also had trouble with my in-laws. And my husband was not so good. That's why I came to Singapore.'

'Wah, such bad luck …' Ma said, shaking her head sympathetically. After a short silence, Helen turned to me.

'What are you going to wear to the wedding?'

Ma sniffed. 'That girl? Hah! She's too lazy to go shopping so she's also going to wear a cheongsam.'

'Ma, you know it's very hard to find dresses to fit me.'

'Cheh, you're just too lazy to look.'

'I can only find clothes to fit me in the children's section! How to find a proper dress?'

'Huh? So difficult?' Helen studied my clothes. I turned to face her so she could see everything and plucked at my clothes 'Girl's jeans and my T-shirt is XS.'

'You look like a small boy.' Ouch!

'Right! Right!' Ma was pleased to have Helen agree with her.

I rolled my eyes. Shopping is a pain when you know that nothing is going to fit you.

Helen pulled at my t-shirt, bunching the extra fabric at the waist to see what was underneath.

'Not bad. I think she'll look good in a cheongsam.'

'You think so?' Ma wasn't so sure. 'How can you tell? When Beng got married, she wore a skirt and blouse. The skirt was so loose it was hanging on her hips. That's why this time I'm choosing.'

'Enough, enough. Ma, do you want anything more to eat? If not, we should go to the tailor's. Otherwise you won't have time to visit with Ah Gu afterwards. Don't forget I have to leave by five o'clock.'

Ma looked down at her almost-empty bowl and decided

that she'd had enough.

'Helen, sorry but we'll go first.' I smiled apologetically as we got up to leave. 'Nice to see you again!'

'Don't give your mother too much trouble, okay?' Helen laughed as she waved us good-bye, then 'Wait, wait! Give me your pager number again!'

I wrote it down for her on another page out of my notebook before I had to scurry off to catch up with Ma.

* * *

I met Jeevan at the Tanglin Gate at five-thirty. He was carrying a backpack, which I'd never seen him do before.

The mystery was solved when we found a spot to sit. He pulled out a folding plastic mat and laid it down on the grass.

'Wah! So well-prepared.' I plopped myself down.

'Of course,' he smiled as he settled himself down beside me and reached into his backpack again and pulled out a flask and two plastic cups. 'I even brought drinks!' He carefully filled a cup and handed it to me.

'Thanks!' I sipped and was happy to find that it was ice-cold rose syrup with lime.

Around us, families were preparing to have a good time, with more elaborate set-ups than Jeevan's.

'Ooh ... picnics,' I said. He looked a bit worried.

'I was thinking we could just eat at Taman Serasi, or if you are up for the walk, Adam Road.'

'Either is okay.'

The sun had started to drop, lengthening the shadows even

though it was still very bright. The stage was in the middle of the lake. There was a buzz of activity as people went back and forth along the single walkway.

'So how was your week?' I asked as we watched the musicians carry their instruments on to the stage.

'Busy. Next week the Science Club will be learning how to conduct a flora and fauna survey in MacRitchie. So this week I've been pestering the students to hand in their signed consent forms.' He rolled his eyes. 'No joke, with Sally's murder still unsolved. I've pretty much had to call all the parents at night to persuade them that their little darlings won't get killed ...'

'Aiyo ... that must be tough.'

I hesitated then asked, 'Do you teach a Tan Yock Li?'

'Tan Yock Li?' He frowned and rubbed his chin. 'No, why?'

'No ... well, it doesn't matter if you don't know her. Anyway, when will the Science Club be doing the survey?'

'Monday and Tuesday. Crossed fingers nobody gets lost in MacRitchie. I'm going to be counting heads constantly!' He sighed then smiled. 'How about you? Any plans for next week?'

'I'm going to see a movie on Monday night with Shanti.'

'Which movie?'

'*Evita* — she's a Lloyd Webber fan.'

'Oh good! I was going to ask you if you wanted to see *Star Wars*.'

'Oh, I already saw that last night with John. I wish you'd mentioned it earlier. You could have come with us —' I felt something change and I turned my head in time to see a flicker of *something* cross his face.

'That's too bad. Maybe I should check with him first the

next time I want to ask you out.'

Wait a minute. Was that sarcasm???

But the musicians were in their seats, the conductor was on his podium and the emcee's voice was booming out the introduction. The concert was starting, and our conversation was over.

It did not resume after the concert. We walked over to Taman Serasi for dinner. We didn't say much. I tried a couple of topics but he didn't seem to be in the mood to talk so we just ate in silence and I went straight home afterwards.

Men are so strange.

16 Mar | Sunday

I was shelving books when Lakshmi came over.

'Ughhh! I'm so bored!' she said as she started to droop against the free-standing shelves. I caught her and pushed so she was leaning against the wall instead.

'Too free, is it? I thought you were busy studying for your O-levels.'

'That's all I'm doing! Study, study, study! I'm sick of studying!'

'Then take a break lah!'

'And do what? My father won't let me go anywhere other than school or the shop. And even at the shop, I have to ask permission to go anywhere. I even had to get permission to come here!' she ended indignantly. Since there was only Matt's shop, Music Matt, between Can-Do and Jaipur Carpets, we are well within earshot, if not eyeshot ... well, we would be if it were any other shop but Matt's.

'That is a bit excessive,' I agreed.

'So, how's Nik doing?' Lakshmi asked, suddenly lifting her head. 'He hasn't been coming to Auntie Rosnah's shop and even at school, he hasn't done more than say "Hi!" and "Bye!" to me,' she pouted.

'Well, your father did tell him to stay away from you. What

did you expect him to do?'

'I didn't expect him to be so obedient!'

I laughed. 'Wah … Juliet is missing her Romeo, is it?'

She sniffed haughtily. 'No lah! It's only that we've been playing together since kindergarten and suddenly he's got no time for me.'

'Don't you have any other friends? How about Yock Li? Or that other girl that came that day — what was her name again?'

She groaned 'Which day? Oh, that day we heard that Sally had been murdered? We're not really friends, you know. I only brought Yock Li because she was so upset — I was trying to distract her. And then that Chloe just followed along.'

I reached up and patted her on her head. It was a bit of a stretch even when she was slouching.

'Such a kind girl — oi! Stop hitting me! I mean it! It really was kind of you to try to distract Yock Li that day! How is she now?'

'Seems normal, I guess. She comes to school, she goes home … I don't talk to her much normally. Different groups.'

'Lakshmi! Where are you?' Uncle Nathan called.

She rolled her eyes but answered 'Here, talking to Mei.' She left, dragging her feet. I shook my head and finished shelving.

* * *

John still had steak on the brain and when he picked me up, I found out that we were going to Fosters.

Fosters was a steakhouse in Specialist Centre. It was a bit dark, but had little oil lamps on every white-clothed table. I guess it was for ambience but I kind of like seeing what I'm eating. Oh well …

The waiter actually seated me. So fancy …. A sort of still life comprising a couple of suits of armour stood in a corner. I wondered if armour was real or fake. I thought I could fit in one of them, it was pretty small.

'I'm feeling rather under-dressed,' I muttered to John.

'Why?'

I rolled my eyes. Typical male. At the other tables, the couples our age were obviously on dates, the girls in dresses and the men in nice shirts and pants. John was looking nicely put together in a white polo and chinos. I, on the other hand, was still in my work jeans and t-shirt. Oh well.

We studied the menu. I nearly choked at the steak prices but happily they had non-steak alternatives which were cheaper. Ooh … cottage pie. That had mashed potato. I love mashed potato!

'Decided?' asked John looking up.

'Yup. I'm having the cottage pie.'

'That's all? Why don't you have a soup or salad? I'm having the lobster bisque.' He flagged a waiter.

'We'd like to order. We're both going to start with the lobster bisque and then she's having the cottage pie and I'll have the pepper steak, medium rare.'

What????

The waiter scribbled in his notebook then asked, 'And for dessert?'

John caught my fulminating eye. 'Umm … let's see how we feel later.'

'If you want the apple pie, that will take twenty minutes.'

'That's all right.'

The waiter went off and I glared at John. 'Lobster bisque?'

'What's wrong? Are you allergic? I can change it to the French onion soup,' and he raised his hand.

'That's not the point. I didn't want a soup.'

'Come on, Mei, don't be like that,' he cajoled. 'I really wanted the soup and I wanted you to try it because it's really good! It's my treat.'

'But —'

'Please ...' He gave me his best coaxing smile. I tried to hold out but ... the lashes won.

'Oh, all right.' Rather ungraciously but I couldn't help it.

The waiter brought dinner rolls and butter to the table. I broke one in half, applied butter and bit into it. Yum ... hot melting butter, a crunchy crust and fluffy insides.

'If you finish your roll now, you won't have any to eat with your soup.'

'I'm really hungry.'

'Maybe we should have gotten a salad as well.'

'No, no. This is fine.'

The waiter brought our soup. I took a spoonful. It smelled like the essence of the sea drowned in butter and alcohol and tasted even better.

'How is it? Do you like it?' John's voice came from far away.

'Ummm ...' My mind was too busy being blown to answer more coherently. I heard him chuckle but ignored him, focusing on enjoying every drop of the soup.

The cottage pie was a more prosaic experience after the

lobster bisque but still good. John passed over a piece of steak which was also pretty good.

My mood was much improved by the time I finished my cottage pie. I smiled at John and he smiled back. 'Dessert?'

'No thanks, I'm stuffed. I'm going to be rolling home as it is.'

'Just a coffee then?'

'Yes, please.' I was starting to feel groggy from the food and maybe the coffee would keep me awake long enough to reach home.

'So, how's things at school?' I asked, trying to keep my eyes open.

'Enh,' he shrugged. 'Normal, I guess'

'Jeevan told me there's still no news about Sally's murder.'

'No, still nothing. But every so often, we get a memo about how we're supposed to look out for any students who are having problems and provide support.'

'Huh.'

'Like it's so easy. Even if the students are told at every assembly that they should come to us if they are having issues, do you think the students will just come up to me and go "Mr Kong! Mr Kong! I've got a problem."'

I chuckled. 'It would make things too easy.'

He rolled his eyes. 'I can't even get them to speak up in class about their views on Romeo and Juliet's family problems so it's highly unlikely that they would tell me anything about their own families.'

The waiter brought our coffees and a small jug of milk. I poured a little into my coffee and watched the light swirl spread slowly through the dark.

'Speaking up is not something we do in Singapore …'

'That's the truth! I really feel it after so many years in the US.'

'I wonder if Sally would have died if she had just spoken to somebody.'

'I wasn't her class teacher, but I should have noticed … done something,' he looked down and added softly, 'if only she had trusted me.'

'I wonder what Sally was doing outside Zouk.'

'Teenagers also go to clubs, you know.'

'Not teenagers her age. For one thing, she was under the age limit and, for another, it's so expensive I doubt she could afford the cover charge.'

'Rich parents?'

'Definitely not rich parents. Her father's a bit of a slimeball. And I gather he doesn't have a steady job.'

John quirked an eyebrow. 'How come you know so much about Sally, Mei?'

Uh oh … what was I thinking?

'I was talking to some of her classmates. Apparently Sally was having to work part-time to support herself.'

John looked stricken. 'Why didn't she say something? Maybe we could have gotten her some financial help.'

'Maybe she thought she was coping fine?'

John scratched his chin. 'If that's the case then it's a good question how she got the money.'

'Mmm.' That was the question that nagged at me. If Sally had left the karaoke lounge, what was she doing to earn enough money to go to Zouk? Although I was working fulltime and living at home, I winced when I heard how much the tickets were. Also, she was underage so ...

'Mei? Mei!' A hand waved before my eyes.

'Huh? Oh, sorry! Could you repeat what you said?'

'I was asking if you like Penang food.'

'Who doesn't?'

'Well, it's my birthday next week, so I was wondering ...' he eyed me cautiously. 'If you would go to the Penang buffet at Princess Terrace with me that Friday.'

I opened my mouth and closed it again. I was feeling a pain in my wallet already. But he'd been buying too often so I really should be reciprocating.

John was watching me as I thought. He looked slightly amused as if he could see the wheels turning in my head.

'Okay,' I finally said. 'On one condition.'

'What condition?'

'I'm paying.'

He opened his mouth but I quickly cut in, 'Non-negotiable.'

He closed his mouth.

'So how?'

'Oh, all right! But,' he added, 'since you'll be buying next time, I'm paying this time.'

He beamed at me, as if he'd gotten one over on me, then called for the bill.

* * *

Lying in bed that night, I realised that I had missed my chance to ask John if he knew Yock Li. Given that the teachers were supposed to look out for students troubled by the murder, why hadn't anybody spotted how miserable she looked? Maybe she was managing to hide her unhappiness better at school? I didn't know.

Should I even be telling anybody at school? Kaypohing is one thing but this was like tattling on her. If she didn't want to seek help at school, maybe she had her reasons. I should just keep out of it.

17 Mar | Monday

I was shelving books in the back of the shop when I heard John greet Auntie Fong.

'Wah! Why so early today?' asked Auntie Fong.

'Term break,' John said. 'Since there aren't any classes, we can finish a bit earlier.'

'So good one! You're going to look for more books, is it? Go, go!'

John laughed then came to me.

'Any recommendations for me?'

I cocked my head to one side thinking.

'What was the last book you read?'

'*The English Patient*. Did you see the movie?'

'No, but I did read the book.' And hadn't liked it. I pondered.

'Do you want something similar or completely different?'

'Hmm ... What are you reading right now?'

I blushed. 'The Anne of Green Gables series. Don't laugh!' John's lips were pressed together and his shoulders shook slightly. 'Somebody returned it, I picked it up and ... now I'm rereading the whole series.'

'I'm not laughing,' he said but his voice shook slightly. I rolled my eyes and turned away from him and continued shelving.

'Don't be mad ...' his voice came from behind me coaxingly. 'I came to see if you wanted to go eat laksa in Katong.'

'Ooh!' I perked up but, 'No ... sorry, I can't go, I already have something on.'

'Who with?'

'I'm going to see a film with my friend, Shanti.'

'Oh well ... how about Wednesday then?'

'Set.'

After he left, Auntie Fong shook her head at me. 'Leng zai wants to take you out and you want to go out with your friend instead. How to get married like that?'

I laughed. 'I've been so busy, I haven't seen Shanti in weeks! I just saw him last night.'

* * *

'So, how's it going with your love life?' Shanti asked. 'Every time I call you're not in.' We were sitting in Capitol Theatre waiting for the film to start.

I hadn't seen or spoken to Shanti for a couple of weeks. What with coaching Nik and going out with John and Jeevan ... Also, I wasn't quite sure what she would say if I told her about my visit to Jimmy Song.

And then there was that MRT incident.

She squirmed in her seat, trying to make herself more comfortable. 'Aiyo! So uncomfortable! Did they think only midgets watch movies?' Her knees were propped up on the back of the seat in front of her and she kind of overflowed her seat. Happily, the theatre wasn't that full so I moved one over putting a seat between us.

'I'm perfectly comfortable,' I smirked.

'Designed for midgets,' she grumbled. 'As I was saying, how's the love triangle going? Have you decided which one yet?'

'What love triangle?'

'Can don't play stupid with me, can or not? You know I mean the two teachers.'

'We're just …' The word "friends" hung on the tip of my tongue. But was that really true? I remembered John holding me as I cried on Friday then holding my hand as we walked to his car and Jeevan's laughing face as he pulled me by the hand towards the river path then that flicker of expression when I told him about going to see a show with John. Much as I wished we were all just friends, somehow I couldn't quite believe it was true.

'What are you thinking?' Shanti asked but just then the lights went down and the ads and trailers started and it was too loud to keep on talking. I heaved a quiet sigh of relief and settled down to watch.

However, Shanti has got a memory like an elephant, she's as tenacious as a bloodhound on the trail and she had no intention of letting me get away without answering her questions. Even as we were walking out of the theatre, her hand on my arm was like a vice.

'What's going on with you and those two?'

I sighed. 'I don't know. I think I want to go back in my room and not come out.'

'You may as well tell me.'

'You remember how you and Yong got together?'

'Me and Yong? What do you mean?'

'You were friends first so you knew each other pretty well before you started going out.'

'Yaaa ... so?'

'Isn't that the way it should be? Instead of jumping in without getting to know each other first? Both of them are acting like ... like ...' I couldn't even get the words out of my mouth.

'Like they want to be your boyfriend?'

'Yaa!!!' I wailed. 'It's not like I'm pretty and charming and they don't really know me so ...'

'You think they have an ulterior motive? You're so paranoid!'

'It's just happening too fast. Even if it was just one person, I'd want them to slow down but now it's two and what with NIE and Sally —' I clapped my hand to my mouth but too late.

'You're still kaypohing around that girl?'

'No, not really.'

'What did you do?' She sounded resigned.

'I err ... went to see her father.'

'What???'

'I just wanted to see what he was like —'

'You really want to die, is it? You're obsessed with this girl! You —'

'Stop, stop, stop! Listen to me!' I pulled at her arm to make her stop. 'Jeevan told me that he, the father, was asking the school when they were going to give him the pek kim — the funeral money. So I called him and said that I wanted to give him the pek kim. Perfectly reasonable ... although he ended up fighting with his girlfriend and throwing the both of us out. And, Shanti, his girlfriend told me that Sally had left her job at the

179

karaoke lounge because she had another job!'

'She was working in a karaoke lounge? She wasn't even old enough to drink!'

'That's just it. Nobody cared about her. Her mother left, her father's a selfish bastard who would take the money she earned, she was being bullied in school …' To my disgust, my eyes started to tear again. Damn. I blinked hard, willing the tears to back up but too late.

'Why are you crying?' Shanti's sharp tones held a note of concern.

'Nothing.' I swiped at my eyes with the back of my finger but it wasn't enough and I had to dig in The Bag for my packet of tissues.

'You're really upset.' Her voice had softened, surprised.

I blew my nose. 'It's just so sad. You never realise how people can just slip between the cracks until you actually see it happen. I mean, it's not just Sally, I think her mother also disappeared. Nobody even reported her missing — I asked Teck Wai.'

She patted my shoulder awkwardly. We started walking again, me still sniffling a little.

'Okay,' she finally said. 'Just promise me you won't do anything stupid.'

'I won't'

'Liar.' She sighed. 'You're such a softie. I really don't know how you're going to survive teaching. The students are going to eat you alive.'

'That's why you love me, right?' I cuddled her arm for a brief moment before she shook me off muttering, 'You don't know what personal space is, is it?'

18 Mar | Tuesday

Teck Wai came to the shop after lunch to collect Auntie Fong for her appointment at the National Eye Centre. She'd been complaining about floaters. The appointment instructions said that she needed somebody to take her home since she wasn't going to be able to see with her pupils dilated.

Just when he showed up, she decided that she really needed to go to the toilet before leaving.

'Five minutes,' she called over her shoulder as she rushed off.

Teck Wai picked up his mother's paper and laid it out on the children's books display to read. I eyed him from behind the counter.

'How's the Sally Song case going?'

He shook his head as he turned a page. 'No good. Everywhere also dead end.'

'Didn't you talk to Yock Li?'

He rolled his eyes. 'Huh. Haven't even finished asking my first question, she's already crying.'

'What did Inspector Rizwan say?'

He shrugged. 'Be patient, try again. He's very busy closing another case so I have to push this one by myself for now.'

I bit my lip. Should I tell him what Helen told me? It didn't really add anything, did it? Just that Sally was having to work to support herself. Also, he was bound to scold me for going to see Jimmy Song, just like Shanti.

Just then, Auntie Fong came back and they left for the appointment.

But I was left feeling unsettled. Torn even. Ai mai? Ai mai? Should I, shouldn't I? The question ran like a thorny refrain through my head the rest of the afternoon. I went through all the motions, paying out on returns, taking money for sales, smiling … on automatic.

I heaved a sigh of relief when I closed up the shop by myself and took myself off home. When you're working, there really isn't that much time to read so I treasure my bus rides to and from work as precious reading time. But this evening, I couldn't focus on the book so I ended up just staring out of the window.

In fictional mysteries, the amateur detective would run around sticking her nose in things and just get a smack on the wrist. That would definitely not work in Singapore. I was more likely to get arrested, not to mention what would happen if Ah Pa and Ma found out. Let's just say that being over 21 might not save me.

But was I okay with just letting the police get on with it, when nobody would tell them anything?

Ma had cooked my favourite dinner: Teochew moi. Her go-to when she was tired of cooking, she only did a chye poh omelette and stir-fried vegetables but added sides of shop-bought pickled mustard greens and a can of fried dace with salted black beans. Those simple flavours with a bowl of hot watery rice porridge were comforting.

I ate in silence, answering Ma's questions with absent ums and ahs. After a while, she gave up and started asking Ah Pa about his day.

I was washing up when she nearly gave me a heart attack by suddenly appearing at my elbow and asking, 'What's wrong?'

The pot I was washing slipped out of my hands and crashed into the sink. Luckily, rice cooker pots are light and there was nothing fragile beneath.

'Nothing's wrong … just thinking about a problem.'

'Don't think so hard. If you don't know, go and ask someone. At the most you'll be a fool for five minutes only.'

* * *

'John? Mei here.'

'Hi Mei! What's up?'

'Sorry but I won't be able to make dinner tomorrow, something came up. Can we do it on Saturday instead?'

'Sure. Nothing serious, I hope.'

'No, no … not serious, just something I have to do.'

19 Mar | Wednesday

After the lunch rush was over, I was FREE! Don't get me wrong. Working at Can-Do is not a hardship. I like the people, I love the books but an afternoon off is priceless. You get to eat somewhere different. Shanti complains that all I ever think about is food. Not true! But I like a bit of variety. Eating the same thing all the time is so boring …

Today, what I wanted to eat was poori. Freshly fried so that it was all puffed up … yum!

It's a straight shot to Little India by the 48 bus. It came quite quickly and it was almost empty. Just before the door closed, Third Girl, I mean Chloe, rushed on.

It was such a surprise, I just stared at her. She looked back at me and flushed red. Then she set her jaw and came to me.

'Can I sit here?'

Wondering what she wanted, I slid in to make room for her. She sat and stared ahead for a while.

'I'm sorry,' she finally said, sounding like the words were being dragged out of her. 'I shouldn't have been so rude to you that day.'

Rude? That was not the word I would have used. More like 'threatening' or 'aggressive' or just a straightforward 'scary'.

'What I don't understand is why. Since you were following

her about, you must know that she came to see me.'

'I was worried. Since Sally died, Yock Li's been acting strange.'

'Oh dear. Strange how?'

She seemed to be searching for words.

'Different.'

Was I so inarticulate at that age? I have no idea.

'Different, how?' Just like pulling teeth.

'She … well, she won't talk to me.' That came out through gritted teeth. I wondered if Yock Li knew that she was spreading at least some of the rumours about Sally.

'Oh dear. Is she talking to anyone else?'

'I don't know. She's avoiding me.'

'Err … well. So where are you going?'

'Erm …' she looked around to see where we were. 'Nowhere in particular.'

'Do you even know where this bus is going?'

No answer.

'So now you're following me, is it?'

'I only wanted to apologize.'

'If that's the case, you could have just come to the shop, right? And how did you know that I'd be leaving early today?'

She pressed the bell. 'Bye.'

'Wait!' But she just got up and went to stand by the exit until the doors opened and she got off.

She's so weird. And it was a bit scary to know that she'd been watching me. How long has she been doing that?

* * *

After that encounter, I didn't feel up to going to Little India after all. So I got off at Empress Market, ate, checked my trusty bus guide then crossed the road to take the 93.

Even though Jimmy wasn't going to talk to me again, I figured it was no harm just going to take a look about the estate. A little run down, I'd heard talk that it was up for redevelopment.

The thing about HDB estates is that all the blocks tend to look alike. The slab blocks looked like they were overdue a fresh coat of paint. The ground floor flats had potted plants lining the outside edge of the drain. There was even a small table and chairs beneath a sunshade. That looked like a nice place to kick back on a Sunday morning.

I found what I was looking for: a coffee shop in one of the blocks.

'Yào hē ma?' called the drinks stall woman as I entered. 'Home-made barley? Lime juice?'

'Ummm …' I went over and studied the menu of drinks behind her. 'One teh-O kosong, please.'

When she brought the tea over, I paid her and commented, 'Very quiet.'

She looked around at the empty shop and shrugged. 'This time of day always like that.'

'Why don't you come and sit with me? Nobody here.'

She shrugged again but came out and joined me at my table, taking a seat that let her see if anybody came in looking for a drink.

'This estate must be quite old, right?' I asked, blowing on my tea. 'I wonder what's going to happen when 99 years is over. Maybe can en bloc soon.'

'Who knows … only gahmen can say right?'

'Got quite a few already, I thought.'

A woman came out from the economy rice stall carrying a plate. A late lunch? She spotted the drinks stall lady and came over to join us.

'What are you talking about?'

'En bloc.'

'This place can en bloc, meh? Nobody wants to stay here. All the flats so old already.'

'That's why maybe time to en bloc.'

Good old HDB — always a good conversation starter. Said conversation got quite animated, a couple of old uncles who came in to drink beer also getting into the action. When it slowed down a bit, I decided to make my move.

'By the way,' I broke in. 'Last time Sally got work here or not?'

'Sally?' said the economy rice lady looking clueless.

'Neh, Sally — that girl who was helping me that time,' answered the drinks lady nudging her.

'Jimmy Song's char bor.'

'Oh … that girl ha?' exclaimed one of the drinking buddies. 'She died, right? I saw in the newspaper.'

'Hoi! So young already dead hor?'

'Killed,' he said, nodding sagely, 'by an ang moh.'

'Uncle ah, how you know it was an ang moh?'

'Hai yah, near that area full of ang moh — all looking for girls. She probably said no and —' he drew his finger gruesomely across his throat.

His quieter friend said, 'She was a good girl. You remember

that boy or not? That one ... he overdosed in the void deck the other day? She was the one who called the ambulance.'

'Really?'

'Yah ... I was coming out of the lift when I heard her on the phone. Then I saw her run away.'

'Huh,' grunted the gruesome uncle but I was wondering how Sally had been so conveniently nearby. Nothing I'd heard about the girl implied she spent any time hanging out at the void deck.

'When was this, uncle?'

He pondered for a bit.

'Bai Tian Gong ah? I think around there.' The 8th day of Chinese New Year. The Hokkien New Year.

That was the week before Sally was found dead.

* * *

I no longer had any doubt that I needed to tell Teck Wai what I'd found out. After washing up the dinner things, I trotted down to the payphone. This was not a conversation I wanted Ma to hear.

'Teck Wai ah? Mei here.'

'Mei? Why are you calling my handphone? It's supposed to be only for work leh.'

'Well, it is for work ... sort of.'

'Huh? What you mean?'

So, I told him about my visit with Jimmy Song, and then my talk with the coffee shop folk and my suspicions.

'Wah piang! You want to die, is it?' He was almost sputtering with indignation. 'How can you just go and talk to Jimmy Song like that? You think you're police, is it?'

'Actually I told him I knew Sally and wanted to give pek kim.'

I could almost hear his eyes rolling in the silence.

'Mei ah, don't play play, can or not? Sally already gone case, then you want to go kacau-kacau like this, you want to die, is it?'

I closed my eyes ... should I tell him about the MRT incident? Probably not a good idea. I didn't even know for sure it wasn't an accident.

'Just promise me you won't go poking around anymore.'

'Promise.'

* Click *

Wah! He never even said 'Thank you'! I glared at the phone. See if I help you anymore!

* * *

Police Cantonment Complex

Teck Wai glared at the phone. Why was she being so kaypoh about this case? She should realise this was police business and she should just keep out of it.

He didn't know which irritated him more, that she was kaypohing around the case or the fact that she managed to find out something he wasn't able to.

'Wah! Your face so scary.' Rizwan dropped a stack of folders on his desk. 'What happened?'

'Mei just called to tell me that Sally may have been involved in drugs,' Teck Wai growled. 'She's been poking around Sally's estate. How the hell did she find out where the girl lived?'

'Drugs?' Rizwan perched on a neighbouring table. 'How?'

'She's not sure. Apparently Sally called the ambulance when a boy overdosed in the void deck and Mei suspects that she may have had something to do with the overdose because she was too conveniently there. According to Mei, Sally was having to work to support herself so it was unlikely that she would be hanging out in the void deck so she says that chances that she just happened to be passing by are very low.'

'Wah! How did she find that out?' Rizwan was impressed.

'Kaypohing lah! What else?' Teck Wai flopped back in his chair and threw his pen on the desk. 'She's been talking to a lot of people including Jimmy Song. I already told her to stop it.'

'Mmm ... that's too bad.' Rizwan rubbed his chin, seeming to fall into a reverie.

'Sir!' Teck Wai was appalled. Rizwan snapped out of it.

'No, no ... you're right to tell her to stop it. Well, we should make the most of the information. You know, durian runtuh cannot waste. Anyway, go and see whether the boy is still alive. Maybe he can tell us something.'

'Yes, sir!'

'Also ask Narcotics if they know anything.'

21 Mar | Friday

I was minding the shop when I got a page from an unknown number. When I called back, it turned out to be Helen.

'Mei, I was just talking to Ah Seng, and he told me that a few weeks ago, Sally came and begged him to lend her some money. Said she would work at the karaoke bar until she had paid him back.'

'Really? When was this?' I heard her call out the question in the background.

'He says it was about three or four weeks ago.'

'So did he give her the money?' Again, she called out the question but this time I heard a growl of 'So kang kor!' and the sound of a receiver being snatched away.

Then a man's gravelly voice came clearly over the line. 'That girl, she want to borrow $20,000! I made of money, is it? She work until die also cannot pay back!' He huffed. 'Don' know what kind of problem she got.'

'$20,000 ah? Wah!' I was gobsmacked. 'Did she say what it was for?'

'I already said I don' know — what kind of stupid question? I asked but she like going to cry. Some more she wanted it right away — who got so much money?'

'Uncle ah, can I tell my friend? He's the inspector trying to

191

find out who killed Sally. Can he come talk to you?'

'Don' want lah! What you think? I so free want to talk to the police? Some more, people see police come sure got problem!'

'Please laa, uncle! He really needs your help.' I thought a bit, 'What if he comes really quietly? If I come with him, we can pretend to be customers …'

'Hah? You also ah?'

'Can or not? Pleeease!'

He thought for a while. Unable to keep still, I got up and started bouncing on my toes. Auntie Fong who just came back stared at me. I stopped. Finally …

'Okay lah.'

'Thank —'

'But,' he continued. 'Only ten minutes and you each have to buy drinks.'

I thought for a bit. 'Can I check with him first? Then I call you back?'

He grunted and hung up.

I hit the switch hook then dialled Teck Wai's handphone number. He picked up almost immediately.

'Ma, what's wrong?'

'Err no, it's Mei.'

'You again … why are you calling me on my handphone? For work only leh!'

'Well, it is for work. Your work, that is, not mine.'

Auntie Fong was staring daggers at me. I could read her mind and it was running along the lines of 'That girl ah … using the phone like free li' dat …' I pinned the receiver between my ear and shoulder, pointed at it, signed 'five minutes' then put my palms together and begged silently.

'What is it?'

'I have a tip for you. Sally asked somebody for a $20,000 loan.'

'Who? How did you find out?'

'I can't tell you unless you agree to his terms.'

'Wah piang! I'm police, you know?'

'Ya but he won't talk to the police. He'll only talk to you if you pretend to be his customer.' I saw Auntie Fong's ears prick up at the word 'police'.

'Undercover?'

'Err … So long as you don't look like police already can. Oh and you have to buy drinks for you and me.' Her head cocked to one side interrogatively.

'Buy drinks for you? Why?'

'Because I said that I'd be going with you. Anyway, I have to go along. He doesn't know your face … actually he doesn't know mine either but Helen does —'

'Mei ah —'

'Yes or no? Quickly answer, can or not? I have to get off the phone — your mother is looking at me.' Auntie Fong's eyebrows shot up.

Teck Wai sighed. 'I have to check with Inspector Rizwan. I'll call you back.' He hung up and Auntie Fong pounced the moment I put down the receiver. As expected.

I was still fending her off ten minutes later when the phone rang.

'Can-Do Bookshop, Mei speaking.'

'Okay. Let me know where and what time.' He hung up.

When I called Uncle Seng to arrange the details, before he hung up he said, 'And Helen said dress nice-nice so people can see that you're a char bor. Otherwise people think got small boy running around for what.'

Great. Everyone's a critic.

* * *

'Hi, John. So sorry but I can't go to Katong tomorrow … Can we postpone again?'

'Again? What's happening? I'm beginning to get the feeling that you don't want to go out with me.'

'No, of course not! I'm … Well, I just have a lot of things going on right now. How about Sunday?'

'Sorry, I have something on that night. How about Monday instead?'

'Monday? I'm coaching Nik that evening. How about Tuesday?'

'Tuesday?' I heard the flipping of pages. 'Look, if you're so busy, let's just shelve Katong for now. We're going to Princess Terrace on Friday anyway. Don't forget.'

'No, I won't forget. I've already made the reservation. I'll see you on Friday then.'

Relieved, I put down the receiver. I felt a bit bad. If I were him, I'd be upset too.

Ma was watching me instead of the TV.

'Is that the teacher?'

I just nodded, too tired to speak.

'Wah, so good one. You better be careful otherwise another

woman will come and snatch him.'

* * *

Police Cantonment Complex

Teck Wai put down the phone and looked across the table at Rizwan.

'Are you sure it's a good idea to have Mei come along?'

'As she said, he doesn't know your face. She'll be your passport.'

Teck Wai sighed and banged his forehead softly on the table.

'She really gets around huh?' Rizwan chuckled. 'I wonder how she found him.'

'More like who told her. Must be that Helen. I think she never met the man before.'

'Who's Helen?'

'I also don't know. She never mentioned her before.'

'Tch tch tch ... she really gets around, ya?' He shook his head admiringly. 'Never mind lah. Before you go see that man we should have a good long talk with Miss Tang Siew Mei. Tell her you'll pick her up say ... one hour early — should be enough time.'

Teck Wai nodded and took a note.

'So how? Did you manage to find the overdose?'

'Still checking.'

'Hmm ...' Rizwan rubbed his chin. 'What did Narcotics say?'

'They haven't got back to me yet. I'll call them again tomorrow.'

'Okay. Let's go over the other cases then. Where are you now?'

22 Mar | Saturday

When I came out of the bedroom, Ma's eyes looked like they were going to fall out of her face.

'What are you wearing?'

'Nice, right?'

I was wearing the black PVC dress that I had bought under Matt's guidance so many days ago and carrying the pair of sparkly stiletto sandals that I'd bought for Ling's wedding. The dress fit, perhaps too well, with cut-in armholes. It couldn't be more different from my normal clothing. I didn't know what to do with my hair so I left it mostly alone, just putting a bit of gel. Looking in the mirror, I felt like something was missing so I dug out a pair of super sparkly earrings, also bought for the wedding, and put them on. Now I felt like a Christmas tree. Maybe I was overdoing it.

Ma circled me like a shark coming in for the kill and then got up close so we were practically nose to nose. I'd tried to replicate the make-up that Matt had done the other night, pretty successfully, I'd thought, so I had major eye liner, eyelashes, and even lipstick.

'Wah! So much make up. Where are you going?'

'Out with Teck Wai.'

'Chan Teck Wai, is it? Why ah?'

'Cannot, meh?'

'You —' But I cut her off when my pager buzzed.

'Sorry, Ma, got to go, he's already downstairs.' I slipped on my sandals outside the door and turned to lock the gate. Ma was already locking it. From the look on her face, I may have raised false hopes.

Teck Wai's jaw dropped when I got into the car. 'You got plasters or not?' I asked. The shoes were a bit big but with the straps pulled to the next to last hole, I'd thought I could manage … if I walked very slowly. But just coming down from the flat, I thought I'd developed a blister even though I'd taken the lift.

'No,' he said, finally getting his jaw under control. 'We can stop and get some at Watson's or Guardian.'

We were leaving early to meet up with Station Inspector Rizwan before heading to Uncle Seng's karaoke bar in Tanjong Pagar.

Station Inspector Rizwan was — wait a minute, that spells 'SIR'! Cool! That's what I should call him for short … 'Station Inspector Rizwan' is too long. I can't think of him as 'Rizwan' — what if I forget and call him that to his face? The good thing about 'SIR' is that even if I forget and call him 'SIR' to his face, he'll only think I'm super polite.

SIR was having dinner in a small makan place down a side street where we joined him. I got nasi padang with kangkong, sambal goreng and, after some thought, asam pedas fish. I eat when I'm nervous.

Unfortunately, I didn't get to eat much of it while the rice was still hot because SIR wanted to know everything.

Everything!

I've never been interrogated like that before. Compared to this, that time I went down to Cantonment could be described as just a gentle questioning. He took me through everything that happened in exhaustive detail from the appearance of the photograph to my call with Uncle Seng.

When I told them about my visit to Crest Motors, the corners of SIR's mouth quivered just the littlest bit before he tucked them in firmly.

'Don't you think it's weird that Mary Wong didn't come forward after the sketch of Sally came out in the papers?' I asked him. 'Maybe something happened to her.'

'Mei, I already told you, nobody reported her missing,' said Teck Wai, exasperated.

'And —' But SIR cut me off.

'Let's focus on Sally right now, okay? We can talk about her mother later.'

I sighed but he was right, so I continued.

SIR was extremely unhappy when I recounted my visit with Jimmy Song.

'That,' he said in measured tones, 'was looking for trouble. Didn't it occur to you that he might be a violent man? You were lucky.' I cringed and Teck Wai gave an 'I told you so' sniff.

He was even unhappier when I described the MRT incident, even though I pointed out that it might have been an accident that I'd blown out of proportion.

When I finished talking, there was a long silence while SIR sipped his kopi reflectively.

Finally, 'What's done is done. You're lucky you didn't get hurt.' He looked meaningfully at Teck Wai. Teck Wai gave him a flat stare back, as if to say, 'What do you expect me to do about it?'

'Anyway,' SIR continued, 'since this man is insisting you have to be there, then no choice, you have to do this. But,' he raised a finger and pointed at me, 'no more digging. Promise?'

I nodded fervently.

It was agreed that Teck Wai and I would go into the karaoke lounge while SIR would wait outside … just in case. We left first then he followed.

As we walked up Duxton Road, I was silently cursing the high heels. Teck Wai, true to his word, had stopped at Guardian and bought me a box of plasters. So I wasn't in pain per se but walking uphill in 6 cm stilettoes is not easy. I teetered and clung to his arm for balance.

The white collars were out and about in the dusk, small groups strolling beneath the streetlights on their way to the bars. I felt a bit awkward and over-dressed among the office clothes. A little like a sarong party girl, except I wasn't with an ang moh.

I was so relieved when we reached the Astara Karaoke Bar & Lounge and I knew I could take the load off my aching feet soon. How such a short distance could feel so long! When we entered, I was a little worried because it was rather dark inside — how would I find Uncle Seng — but he had said that he would be at the bar.

Someone was singing a sad Hokkien song and the big screen TV showed a crying girl walking beneath flowering trees. Amazing how some people can cry so prettily. Of course, she was probably faking it.

I caught sight of Helen sitting at a table with a very happy man. She saw me too and smiled approval of the outfit before she looked towards the bar and nodded at the man standing in front of it. Ah Seng or rather Uncle Seng, I presume?

Uncle Seng was forty, maybe fifty years old, a small trim man, very tanned with his hair slicked back in a pompadour. His shirt was very white, open at the neck and firmly tucked into tight trousers. He came around from behind the bar smiling broadly.

'Ah Mei aaa … so you finally brought your boyfriend to meet me!'

He put his arm around my shoulders and shook Teck Wai's hand. I stiffened slightly but forced myself to relax — this was, after all, what we had agreed. Teck Wai smiled and when Uncle Seng released me, he put his hand on the small of my back and steered me to the corner of the bar where we all perched on bar stools, with me between the two men.

'What drink you want?'

Teck Wai ordered a beer and I asked for a vodka lime.

'So, what you want to know? I very busy, you know.'

'When did Sally start working for you?'

'Last year?' He screwed up his eyes and scratched his chin. 'Hungry Ghost Month?'

'How long did she work here?'

'Maybe one, two months only. So useless. Couldn't even sweet talk the uncles properly.'

'Mei told me that Sally wanted to borrow $20k from you. When was this?'

'After Chap Goh. I think it was Friday, is it?' He pulled a diary out of his back pocket and flicked through it.

'What exactly did she say?'

'Ah! My memory not so good.' Uncle Seng squinted his eyes in an effort to remember. 'She came in the afternoon so when I saw her, I asked her why she wasn't in school. She never answered. Instead she asked if she could borrow $20k. Twenty thousand neh! Wah! I was so surprised.'

'She didn't say what she needed it for?'

'No.'

'Did she say what she wanted it for?'

'Hai ya! I already said no! I asked but she never say. Just looked at me like goondu only.' He sighed. 'Kiā kiā. Donno what kind of shit she kena … Maybe drugs? Twenty thousand dollars not kuching kurap, neh!' He shrugged. 'So much money, must be drugs.'

'So did you give her the money?'

'What you think I am? Made of money, is it? I gave her a hundred dollars and now I'm not going to get it back. Time up.' He got up to go.

'Uncle Seng, ah! One more question, can or not?' He paused and turned to look at me.

'Quickly!'

'Got anybody target Sally or not?'

He gave a short harsh laugh and jerked his chin to indicate the couples and groups scattered throughout the dimly lit room. 'Stupid question. Everybody here kena target, for money, for sex, you name it.'

He signalled the bartender to give us the tab and stalked off to join a table of red-faced men and laughing women.

'Let's go,' Teck Wai said and helped me down off the bar

stool. He looked at the bill and blenched but paid it, taking the receipt and sticking it in his wallet. 'Hope I can claim.'

As we walked out, Helen caught my eye, smiled and waved. I waved back.

SIR shadowed us from the five-foot-way across the road until we were a few storefronts away before he crossed the road to join us at the junction.

We went back to the small makan shop. Going downhill in stilettos is actually worse than going up. My feet were killing me.

'So,' SIR said when Teck Wai finished reporting. 'He thinks it's tied to drugs.'

Teck Wai shrugged.

'I checked the hotline records and found the boy. Turns out he didn't die. I managed to talk to him this afternoon. It was ecstasy. He described the pills as looking like Panda candy, which could tie it to the murder and he identified the photo of Sally as the girl who sold them to him. I also spoke to Narcotics and they gave me a list of drug rings they're looking into. Hmm … maybe I should —' He pulled out his notebook and pen then started to write something down.

I turned to him in surprise. 'Panda candy? What's it got to do to the murder?'

'Sally was found lying on a lot of Panda candy,' he answered absently as he scribbled.

SIR cleared his throat and looked meaningfully at Teck Wai. He looked up, flushed and said 'Oops! Forget I said that.'

SIR turned to look at me and I immediately held up my hands in surrender 'I won't say a word. Promise.'

23 Mar | Sunday

After the excitement of my little venture into the seedy world of karaoke bars and police business, Sunday morning was something of a let-down. We opened later. People were more interested in sleeping in, not having to rush to get kids to school or themselves to work … mostly.

So, despite getting up a bit later, I still had time to drop by the snack shop to browse. Fish crackers were Auntie Fong's favourite and I always want sticky-sweet, spicy-hot chilli belinjo chips. Ooh … they had the little pineapple jam sandwich cookies. About the diameter of a twenty-cent coin, a couple were just right to curb a case of mulut gatal, as Auntie Rosnah would put it.

While I was at the cashier, I saw a display of Panda candy and picked up a packet. It's a great way to wake up a late-night study session or a sleepy Sunday afternoon. I bought a packet and immediately tore it open. Its strong sweet-sour lemon-lime scent filled my nostrils when I popped one in my mouth. The first moment is always the best. Tart enough to make any mouth pucker, the sour cuts through any fuzziness in the brain.

When I got to the shop, Auntie Fong was already there, talking to Jeevan. When he saw me, he smiled tentatively.

'How was the survey?' I asked as I handed Auntie Fong my

bag of goodies.

'Tiring.'

'I can imagine.' I unlocked the shutter and pulled it up. 'Hold on a minute.' I pulled out the display rack of postcards then went in and switched on the lights. Auntie Fong followed me in and went behind the counter to put her bag and the snacks down.

'I was wondering —' he started.

'Sorry but you need to move back a bit, please.' I waved him back a pace then pushed out the display of children's books.

'I —' but now that I had space to manoeuvre, I was pulling out the rack of travel guides.

'Sorry, Jeevan, but can you come back in fifteen — no, twenty minutes? I really need to finish opening up the shop first.'

He gave in. 'Okay. Do either of you want a coffee or something? I can buy for you.'

Auntie Fong quickly said, 'No need, no need. Mei can go have coffee with you. When you come back in twenty minutes.'

'Thank you, Auntie! I'll be back.' He left.

I put down The Bag and eyed Auntie Fong narrowly. She tried giving me the innocent look, failed then said, 'So poor thing. He was already waiting ten minutes when I came. He didn't know we open later on Sunday.'

She clapped her hands. 'Quickly open then can go.'

I quickly ran the feather duster over the books and swept the floor. Luckily no sticky spots today so when Jeevan returned, I was ready to go, wallet in hand, pager in pocket.

'Thanks again, Auntie,' he said to Auntie Fong and waved as we left. Auntie Fong waved back. 'Not too long aaa!' she called after us.

'Hawker centre?' He shrugged assent.

We walked in silence. Down the stairs, through the lobby and out the door. Past the racks of magazines and international newspapers of the newsagent. The sunshine was hot and losing its morning yellow for the white of noon and the five-foot-ways were full of people.

Through the chain link fence, I could see the market was full. No languid crowd, this. These people were out to buy. I could hear sellers crying their wares while the shoppers called out their orders as we walked along the fence.

When we stepped through the narrow gate, I could see the hawker centre was also full. The queue for the economy noodle stall was snaking and most of the tables were full of families either already eating or waiting for their food.

'Let's go somewhere else,' I said.

So we left and walked on until we stood under a shady old tree.

'This is as good as it gets today. Everywhere else is going to be crowded too.' Then I waited. 'What's up?'

For a couple of minutes, he struggled for words. Then he said, 'I like you.'

'I like you too.' So …?

'No, Mei. I LIKE you,' he said meaningfully.

And then it sank in and I remembered the uncomfortable way last Saturday's outing ended.

I froze. What to say? I didn't know what to say. I didn't know if I LIKEd him back. Didn't he think it was a bit fast? I only met him, what, two weeks ago?

'Err …' What was he expecting me to say? 'Ummm …' So awkward! What to say? There are teenagers better at handling this kind of thing than I am. 'I think I need to get back to the shop.' I was so running away.

His face fell but he said with some grace, 'I'll walk you back.'

We walked back in silence. I felt really bad. I've never told anyone that I LIKEd them before. After a couple of mad infatuations, my romances have all been one-sided because I'm too much of a coward to declare myself.

To be honest, unrequited love is so much easier. You yearn, you sigh wistfully and write about it. Then when it's over, it's clean. No hurt feelings to manage, no embarrassment, just a gentle, warm nostalgia when you see a past love.

I suppose it would be mean not to give him an answer. Did I like him? Yes. Did I LIKE him? Dunno …

So how?

Just before we reached Can-Do I stopped him.

'Look, I don't know what you expected me to say but this is all a bit too fast for me.'

I did a quick check to see if he was listening.

Yes, he was. So was Matt, unabashedly, leaning on a CD rack nearby. I made shooing motions at him but he only grinned at me. I pulled Jeevan away from him, nearer to Qurayes Fashion. Safer only because Auntie Rosnah was busy inside with a customer.

'I mean, we only met two weeks ago and I still hardly know you. And frankly, you barely know me.' Still listening. 'Why don't we just hang out for a bit? I'll introduce you to my friends.'

'So, you just want to be friends.' His voice was carefully

neutral.

I sighed. This is so hard.

'I don't believe in love at first sight. I'm not even sure I believe in romantic love.' What a cringe-inducing conversation. Why was he making me do this? 'I like you. But whether I'll ever LIKE you?' I shrugged. 'I don't know. Only time will tell.' There, take it or leave it. If he didn't want to be friends, so be it.

* * *

'Hi Mei.'

Surprised, I looked up from the cash register to see Teck Wai standing at the counter.

'Oh hi! What are you doing here?'

'I'm going for dinner with my mom.'

'Really? I thought —'

'Wah, you're here early!' called Auntie Fong as she hurried back. 'We were just about to start closing up.'

'Auntie Fong, if you want —'

'It's okay if Ah Wai comes? We just go and eat, no reservation, right?'

'But —'

'And he can drive us there and can take you home afterwards. Come, let's close up quickly.' No argument allowed.

We closed up shop then Auntie Fong slipped a hand in each of our arms and towed us to the carpark, chattering happily all the way.

It's always interesting watching them together. When I first started coming to Can-Do, I thought Teck Wai was something of a sourpuss, kind of snooty and stand-offish. Then as I got to know him better, he loosened up a bit but mostly he still seems like he's got a stick up his behind. It's only when Auntie Fong is around that he seems fully relaxed.

Is it because she's his only family?

I got into the back seat and listened to Auntie Fong tell him about her day. I wanted to ask him if the information that Uncle Seng gave him was helpful but (a) I didn't want to interrupt Auntie Fong and (b) I didn't think he would tell me with her there anyway. So I leaned back and just listened as I watched the lights go by.

Finding parking in Geylang is never easy. Teck Wai couldn't find a spot nearby so he dropped us off at the restaurant and went off to try elsewhere.

'Three people,' Auntie Fong told the man as we walked in. There were brightly coloured pictures of their signature dishes on the walls. We got a small table by the wall and studied the laminated menus.

By the time Teck Wai joined us, Auntie Fong had ordered. Not only did she order two types of frog porridge, the white Cantonese style and kung pao, the one with the frog fried with dried chillies served separately, but also baby octopuses (octopi?) deep-fried until crispy in a sticky sweet sauce, crispy roast pork, stir-fried sambal sweet potato leaves and steamed luffa with tofu. When I protested that it was too much food, she only said 'Sure can finish one. Ah Wai eats a lot.'

By the time all the food came, the table was covered with barely any place for our bowls and side plates. Teck Wai shook his head in resignation and set about eating and I followed suit.

Auntie Fong smiled happily but, after her first bowl of porridge, she asked, 'So, Mei, when are you going to start at NIE?'

'July.' I thought a bit. 'Wah! Seems very soon. Maybe we should start looking for somebody to take my place.'

'Hai ya! Got four months more. No rush lah! Worst comes to worst, I can handle myself.'

'Ma, if you get somebody sooner then Mei can help train.'

'Eh, what you think? I don't know how to do things, is it? I ran the bookshop for so many years by myself, you know?'

Teck Wai rolled his eyes. 'Ya, ya …'

His mother sniffed then moved on. 'So how is Siew Ling's wedding coming on?'

'Like that lor. She's quite ngiao. Some more, now audit season.' I shook my head in resignation. 'Quite jialat but what to do? The fortune teller gave three dates, all also around the same time so boh pian.'

'Wah!'

Teck Wai snorted. 'They still believe in this kind of thing meh?' he asked in disbelief.

'Oi! Why you so like that? Can don't be so rude, can or not? Shy only!' His mother glared at him but I laughed.

'I don't think she and Alex care but my mom is very superstitious; her father's family were fishermen before he started selling fish, you know. Beng also had to have the fortune teller pick dates but at least his not so bad — got space between.'

'So when you get married, you also have to go see the fortune teller.'

'Ya lor,' I chuckled. 'If I get married.'

'What do you mean "if"?' Auntie Fong scolded me. 'You're

still young, you know? You need to start looking, otherwise how to find?'

Teck Wai chuckled which he hastily converted to a cough when his mother turned on him.

'And you! When ...'

Hastily he picked up the plate of sotong and pushed some onto her side plate. 'Ma! The sotong is very nice. Eat some more.'

'Enough! enough!' Distracted from her diatribe, she fended him off.

For the rest of the meal and through the dessert we had in a nearby tong shui shop, he kept her distracted with silly stories from when he was on the beat. I particularly enjoyed his story about having to chase a pickpocket down Orchard Road.

By the time I got home, I was tired from laughing. Who knew he could be funny?

24 Mar | Monday

Nik and I were sat in a corner next to the fence in the hawker centre. It was evening and the sun was low on the other side so all we had was the reflected light off the shophouses across the road.

Although his written English was fine, Nik tended to lapse into Singlish when speaking. This would not do for his oral exam. So, while we waited for the lights to come on, we decided to do some English oral practice.

'Nik, have you seen Lakshmi recently?'

'Only in school. I think her father is still m– angry with me. He glares at me whenever he sees me, and Lakshmi hasn't been spending time in the shop.'

'Is there anything you can do about it?'

'Donno —'

'I don't know.'

'I don't know what to do.'

'What does your mother say?'

Suddenly Lakshmi plopped herself on the seat next to Nik. He jumped and turned to look at her in surprise.

'Oi! What are you doing here?' He looked around wildly. 'Where's your father?'

'I've had it with him! I've apologised and apologised and

still he's mad. He calls every thirty minutes to make sure I'm at home! So irritating!'

'Well, you are his only daughter, the apple of his eye, the milk in his tea …'

She sniffed.

'If he wants his only daughter to love him, he's going to have to be more reasonable.'

'If you love someone set them free,' Nik sang.

'Wow, Nick! I didn't know you were a Sting fan!'

'So how?' Nick caught my eye. 'So, what are you going to do about this, Lakshmi?'

'Huh? Why are you talking like that?'

'Nik's practising for his English oral.'

'What??? I need to practice too! See what he's depriving me of?'

Nik cleared his throat and then, in his idea of what an English accent sounds like, said, 'To be fair, my dear, if your father hadn't stopped us from studying together, I too would not be practicing my spoken English thusly.'

Lakshmi smacked him on his arm.

'Violence, violence.' I shook my head. 'Look, obviously there's something going on with your father here.'

'Tell me about it,' she grumped.

'Let's go over the possible reasons.'

'He wants to make my life a misery.'

I shook my head.

'He's a control freak.'

Unexpectedly, Nik put in. 'You're his only daughter and he's afraid something will happen to you.'

Lakshmi and I looked at him in surprise and he blushed but continued.

'That's what my Mak said. Especially after what happened to Sally, and they still don't know who killed her. When you didn't come home for dinner, he probably thought you were dead in an alley somewhere.'

He pondered for a while then said, 'Ya... that's probably it.'

Lakshmi sighed. 'I wish they'd had more children. Then maybe they wouldn't be so focused on me.'

I laughed. 'Maybe but you've still got to live with it. Talk to him. Find out what his concerns are, then maybe you can strike a deal ...'

Lakshmi rolled her eyes but agreed it was worth trying.

'Don't mention me aaa?' Nik cautioned. 'He's still mad at me.'

'Talking about Sally, have you heard anything about how she got killed?'

'No. I never heard anything,' Nik said. 'Eh, I need another drink. Lakshmi, you want?'

She shook her head, he went off then she turned to me.

'Mmm ... not so much. Although Yock Li seems to be a bit less angry ...' Lakshmi twirled a piece of hair around her finger.

'But ...?'

'She still seems stressed. Even though I know that she's started partying again.'

'Partying?'

'Oh ya ... Yock Li really likes to go dancing. She goes to clubs, maybe once or twice a week.'

'Wah, her parents let her? Wait, how do you know she goes

to clubs?'

She shrugged. 'The stamp on the back of the hand — you know, the one for re-entry? I saw it on her hand again. When ah?' She looked up, eyes screwed shut as she thought then, 'Thursday.'

I sat back in amazement. Lakshmi was pretty observant for her age.

'Now that I think about it,' Nick, sitting down again, mused as he bit on his straw. 'I think I saw stamps on Sally's hands a couple of times too. Does it look like this?' He picked up his pen and sketched an elaborate 'Z'.

'How did they get in? They're below the age limit,' I mused. 'Wait a minute. How do you know what the club stamp looks like?'

Lakshmi promptly zipped up her mouth and twinkled like mad. I rolled my eyes and another question crossed my mind.

'Also where was Sally getting the money?'

Lakshmi immediately saw where I was going.

'Ya! Especially if she was having to work part-time. Maybe she was working to get money to go to clubs?' She considered her words then shook her head. 'I didn't think she was the type, you know.'

'What type was she?'

'The stressed type. You know, only average, not exam smart so always mugging.'

'Hard to imagine her and Yock Li being close — you know, the mugger and the party girl.' She shrugged. 'Maybe they've known each other a long time, probably since primary school.' We fell silent and suddenly the cold white light of the fluorescent tubes came on. I checked my watch 'Wah! Already 7 pm?'

Lakshmi leapt up and dashed off without a word. It would not do to be late for dinner again, especially if she was going to be negotiating with her father.

I turned to Nik. 'Back to Geography?'

26 Mar | Wednesday

'So, what are you doing this afternoon?' Auntie Fong asked as was her habit.

'Ummm … maybe Little India. I was supposed to go last week but something came up and I didn't go.'

'What for? I don't know why you go there all the time.'

I looked at her and laughed. 'That's where the best Indian food is, of course!'

'I don't know what's so great about Indian food,' she sniffed.

'It's sour, salty, bitter and got all kinds of spices,' I said, mouth already starting to water. 'I think I'm going to have poori today. I wanted last week but didn't go.'

'What's that? Is it like prata?'

'It's a kind of deep-fried bread. When they fry it, it puffs up so it's like a ball when they serve it hot. Ah … it's so good!'

'Really?' Auntie Fong was intrigued.

'One day we should go and eat together before opening the shop.'

'Can, can!'

I finished packing The Bag and waved goodbye.

Matt was playing Van Morrison's 'Moondance'. I can never resist it and, with a free afternoon ahead of me with no place to be at any particular time, I could and did stop in to enjoy.

When it ended, I heaved a sigh of satisfaction and smiled at Matt.

'That was beautiful. It always makes me happy.'

'Me too. Where are you going? Out with the leng zai?' He smiled mischievously. It's amazing that Matt seems to hear everything we say, given he's usually got music playing. If I didn't know better, I'd think he had us bugged. Or maybe we talk really LOUDLY! I made a mental note to turn down my volume.

'No lah … he's working today. Teacher mah … cannot take leave on school day.'

'He's quite the party boy, you know. Cannot imagine how he can work all day like that and party at night.'

'Really? You do it also, right?' I knew that Matt would sometimes DJ at clubs.

'That's also work for me, you know? And those days I close early and take a break.'

That's work ethic for you. Work all day and then some more at night. Adult life.

I couldn't imagine going out clubbing after a full day at work and then going to work again the next day more than once in a while. The night after we were at Zouk, I'd been dragging around the bookshop so much that Auntie Fong was chochoking me about being as old as she was. I was a bit surprised about John being a party boy, though. I'd imagined he was spending most nights marking like Sharm.

'You see him a lot at clubs, meh?'

'On and off lah. I only started noticing him after he started coming … and coming,' he teased. I rolled my eyes.

'Was he with anyone?' No, I wasn't jealous, was I? It would

be strange if he was by himself in a club.

'Nobody I know.'

'Hmm …' But my stomach growled, reminding me of my poori plan and I made a quick goodbye and left.

Nobody followed me onto the bus this time. Chloe should be back at school so I was reasonably confident that I was unobserved. It was creepy to think that she'd been watching me. I like my privacy …

I wondered how the investigation was going. I hadn't heard anything from Teck Wai but that wasn't a surprise. I hoped that if they caught the murderer, Yock Li would be able to move on. It must be terrible to know your friend was murdered. Beside a club. Maybe even while I was dancing?

My mind drifted to John. He'd never mentioned that he liked to go clubbing to me. Could be that he was there because of the students that were going clubbing, like Yock Li and Sally, trying to keep them out of trouble? That would be above and beyond the call of duty.

Or maybe he just liked to dance.

* * *

Alexandra Secondary School

'Hello?' The woman's voice was sharp and impatient.

Meera took a calming breath, tapped her ball pen twice on the notebook then asked, 'Is that Mrs Tan? I'm Meera Kunasekaran, the Student Welfare Officer from your daughter's school.'

'What is it about this time?'

'This is the third day she hasn't come to school. Are you aware of this?'

'Of course I know! I already told you yesterday.'

'Told me, Mrs Tan? This is the first time I'm calling you.'

'Your colleague lah, that man. He called me yesterday. I already told him Yock Li was arrested! They say she was selling drugs! How can? My daughter's a very good girl, you know?' Meera dropped her pen.

'S-sorry Mrs Tan, can you repeat that?' she asked as she picked up her pen again.

'How can you make me say it again??? I've told you so many times already. I'm very upset, you know? Then you make me repeat over and over again. You are literally causing me pain, you know! Why are you being so cruel to me? I'm going to report you to the police! What's your name?'

'Er … Meera? I'm really from Alexandra Secondary School, you know?'

'Give me your number.'

Meera gabbled her number and quickly ended the call. She hurried to the principal's office, knocked on the door and, without waiting for an answer, flung the door open.

The principal and vice-principal looked up at her in surprise.

'One of our students has been arrested!'

Both men blanched. The principal was the first to speak.

'What happened?'

Meera recounted her conversation with Mrs Tan, concluding, 'It was so weird, how she kept insisting she had spoken to the school already.'

'First the dead girl, now this,' the principal sighed. 'We need to do damage control. Can't have people blaming us for the student — what's her name again?' The principal looked up at Meera who obliged: 'Yock Li, Tan Yock Li.'

'Need to make sure none of the teachers talk to reporters,' the vice-principal said firmly.

'Or any of the students. Meera, can call Agnes please?'

Agnes popped her head out from behind Meera. 'What?'

'Can arrange an urgent staff meeting? I think,' he checked his watch, 'in one hour. Get all the teachers and all the support staff also.'

'So fast one ah?' Agnes turned to go but stopped when he called her back.

'Wait, wait, wait! Do we have assembly tomorrow?'

'No lah! Tomorrow is Thursday leh, where got?'

'Then arrange, can?'

Agnes rolled her eyes in response then took off.

'Meera, give her a hand.' Relieved, she nodded and followed, leaving the two men looking at each other.

'What to do with the parents? When the newspapers find out, sure kena sai,' said the vice-principal, shaking his head.

27 Mar | Thursday

'Mei! You'll never guess!!!'

I was shelving books when Lakshmi came flying in after school.

'Guess what?'

'Yock Li's been arrested!'

'What???' I walked to the front of the store to join her in front of the counter. Auntie Fong who had been reading the paper, stood up and leaned forward.

'Who's Yock Li?' she wanted to know.

'You know lah ... Sally's friend.' I turned back to Lakshmi. 'Arrested for what?'

'Selling drugs!'

'What??? How did you find out?'

'They called a special assembly to tell us — actually they wanted to tell us that if we are arrested for any reason we would be suspended pending expulsion if we are found guilty.'

'So, what did they say?'

'Not much lah. Just that a student had been arrested. And then a whole lot on how the school frowns on drug abuse, anything to do with drugs. Oh and don't talk to reporters.' She grinned. 'They repeated that sooo many times!'

'Wah, they must be having a bad time right now! Wait, they

didn't mention her name? How did you know then?'

'Huh? Oh, we guessed. She hasn't been in school for a couple of days and the teacher just skipped her name when checking attendance today.'

'Wah!' I wondered how they managed to catch her in the act.

'Ya! I'm surprised they're not doing blood tests on all of us. First Sally is killed, now Yock Li is arrested. Must be some kind of link.'

* * *

When I stepped out of the shopping centre after work, Chloe was waiting for me.

'It's all your fault!'

'You again? Anyway, what's my fault?'

'Yock Li's been arrested!'

'How can that be my fault?' Well … actually it could be my fault. After all, I'm the one who told Teck Wai that Yock Li was close to Sally. 'Anyway, why was she arrested? Do you know?'

For the first time, she looked uncertain. 'I … don't know.'

'If you don't know even know why she was arrested, how can you be so sure it was my fault?' I asked reasonably.

She glared at me, still fuming. 'I just know it was you!'

'Ugh! Grow up.' I turned my back on her and stalked off.

I may have left her behind me but I could feel her glare on my back like it was a physical touch. While I was waiting at the bus stop across the road, she was still watching, still glaring. I was relieved when my bus came while she was on the other side of the road. I didn't want her to follow me home. Just to be sure, I stayed on the lower level and watched her watch me go by as the bus carried me away.

Once the bus was well away from Chloe, I scooted up the stairs and flopped down on the front seat. Not a popular seat for tall people because of the limited leg room but that's where you get the best view. I stared unseeing out the window while my thoughts went round and round.

I wanted to call Teck Wai, but I already knew he wouldn't tell me anything; he'd probably scold me instead, so no point.

Uncle Seng had tied Sally's death to drugs. If Lakshmi was right and Yock Li's arrest was related to drugs then that was a line that connected her to Sally's death. But given how upset she was the day Sally's death was announced, it didn't seem like she had known that Sally was dead. Unless she was an award-winning actress. Could she have been faking it?

It just seemed like there were still missing pieces in this puzzle. And nobody knew yet why Sally was killed. And then there was the Panda candy that was scattered around her. Was it a drug deal that went wrong? That the ecstasy pills that Sally had sold to that boy looked like Panda candy, did seem to point to that.

How on earth did Sally and Yock Li get recruited as drug peddlers in the first place? Where would they meet a drug dealer? I really couldn't see one coming up to them on the street and going, 'Hi there! Wanna sell drugs for me?'

Or a sign up outside a shop: 'Drug peddlers wanted.' Ridiculous. This is Singapore. You could get a death sentence just for having enough of the stuff.

It had to have been somebody they knew. Might it have been someone Sally met at Uncle Seng's? Or a friend of Jimmy's?

I sighed. All this thinking was giving me a headache.

28 Mar | Friday

I hate to say it but I had been looking forward to going to the Penang buffet. When we were kids, Ah Pa would take us to Penang during the school holidays. I think sometimes that Penang is how Singapore might have been before Independence. Chaotic, narrow streets with lots of traffic. Old shophouses, a little run down but the best part, to me anyway, is the food. Penang food is really the best. With Chinese, Malay, Indian and Thai influences all mixed together, it really is the original fusion food. Basically we would just eat and eat and eat before buying all the snacks to bring back to Singapore.

Unfortunately, once Beng started to work, and then Ling started, it became harder and harder to find a good time to go. Without them it was just less fun so we finally stopped going. But I really missed the food.

When John picked me up, he was subdued and not saying much for most of the drive.

'Are you feeling okay?' I finally asked. 'If you're not feeling well, we can always cancel.'

'No, no, I'm feeling fine!' he said immediately. 'It's just … did you hear? A student just got arrested.'

'I heard about that! Do you know why?'

'Something to do with drugs,' he sighed then, 'I don't want

to talk about it.'

'Mmm …' I restrained myself from asking more questions.

'What?' He took his eyes off the road to shoot me a quick look then chuckled. 'You're dying to ask more questions, aren't you?

'Noo … yes. Do you think it had something to do with Sally?'

He was silent a long time. 'Why do you think so?'

'Well … I did talk to Yock Li a couple of times, and it seems like she and Sally were close. So for her to be —'

'Yock Li? How did you know it was Yock Li that was arrested? I didn't tell you the student's name.'

I was a little surprised at his vehemence.

'Wasn't it her? That's what her classmate told me.'

'Oh,' he sighed then laughed. 'We've all been told not to divulge any information so I got a shock when you knew her name.'

I smirked and, rubbing my hands together in true villain style said, 'I have my sources.'

* * *

At the buffet, the waiter seated us but we immediately got up to join the hordes at the selections. The char kuay teow was all gone, leaving only a banana leaf with sad bits of kuay teow and grease. The queue at the window for noodle soups was too long for my rumbling tummy to countenance so I helped myself to some rice, a banana leaf-wrapped packet of otak-otak, fried prawn paste chicken and some of the chap chye.

There was only one old man at the pot of too-thor th'ng so I got in line behind him. That steaming peppery soup is one of my favourites. Unfortunately, he was trying to scoop out every ginkgo nut in the pot. Luckily I spotted them bringing out a fresh batch of char kuay teow and managed to be first in line to take a good helping of the steaming noodles.

There was very little conversation at our table other than an occasional 'You gotta try this.' I had multiple bowls of the asam laksa which is my favourite meal in Penang, narrowly edging ahead of their char kuay teow. I don't know what it is that makes it so addictive. Was it the sour-spiciness of the fish soup enhanced by the pieces of pineapple or funkiness of the hae ko that they drizzle over it?

John went back to the buffet a few times for more kueh pie tee and bowls of the Hokkien mee and fried porridge. I assembled some fruit rojak to share and we finished off with some Nyonya kueh. But I just had to have a go at the DIY ice kacang and it was so much fun! Even though I was stuffed by then, I still managed to finish it. Mostly water anyway.

As a result, I was so full when we finished, there was no way I was getting back into the car immediately so I persuaded John to go for a walk around the area. It was a beautiful night, with a slight cool breeze blowing off the Singapore River.

We crossed the road and turned onto the path that ran along the riverbank. Instead of turning right, I turned left to go upstream. We walked past a construction site and then we were passing behind Zouk. I came to a stop. Zouk comprised three big former warehouses and had doors facing the river where they would load and unload goods from the boats that moored there.

A white picket fence cordoned off a narrow strip bordering the river facing side.

As I looked around, a feeling of sadness for the lost girl descended on me. I wondered where she was killed. There was a clump of trees between the construction site and the club. A discreet space for dark deeds but I really couldn't see a teenaged girl willing to hazard that area in the dark without a pressing reason.

'What's up?' John asked turning back to me.

'Nothing really,' I said, turning to walk back towards the construction site. 'It's just that I think Sally was killed around here.'

'Now that you mention it, I think it must have been.'

'I can just imagine it. She meets with the man —'

'I can't believe how ghoulish you're being. Wait, how do you know it was a man? Maybe it was a woman.'

'Okay, okay …' I replied absently. I wondered if there was a way through the trees.

'Do you know if you can get to the front side through those trees? I wonder if a lot of people pass through there. It should be relatively quiet. What do you think?'

'What about?'

'That could be where Sally was killed.' I pointed at the clump of trees. 'On the other side of those trees.'

'Could be.'

'She must have had an appointment with her killer there,' I mused. 'What other reason would she have to be there? Let's go take a look!'

Without waiting, I scrambled up the small slope and plunged

in among the trees. Good thing I was wearing jeans and closed shoes. The brush that grew between the trees was pretty thick.

I pushed my way through and found myself in an alley between the club's wall and the construction site's fence. It was rather dark, at least as dark as it ever gets in Singapore with all its ambient light. I could still make out John's face in the light that came through the mouth of the alley.

Teck Wai said that Sally was suffocated. Did the murderer hold her nose and mouth shut? That seemed a bit difficult. I put my hand over my nose and mouth. Maybe if you had bigger hands. Or if you had a grip on her head with both hands. But then how would you keep a hold of her? Let's see, if you used your body weight to hold her in place ... maybe against the wall?

Even so, if Sally was struggling, it would be difficult to keep a grip on her nose. What with the sweat and all ... it would be like trying to keep hold of a greasy fishball. Maybe if you had gloves on? But who wears gloves in Singapore? Might it have been a random killing by a construction worker? But the construction site was deserted, not a sound to be heard.

It would be much easier to put a plastic bag over her head. Little kiddies do it all the time. But who has a plastic bag handy at a club? I didn't remember seeing Sally carrying a plastic bag at the club.

Maybe Sally didn't come to the club alone. Unless the murderer brought a plastic bag with the intention to kill.

'Do you think Sally came to the club by herself?'

'I don't know.' His voice sounded a bit strange, and I turned to him enquiringly. He did not look well. Sort of sweaty.

'Are you feeling okay? I know I'm being a bit ghoulish ...'

'I'm okay.' He swallowed. 'I think I ate too much just now. Feeling a bit sick.'

'Oh, no! Do you want something sour to suck? I have something here.' I dug about in The Bag and finally, triumphantly, pulled out my already opened packet of Panda candy. I unrolled the top and held it out to him.

He got a whiff of the candy and turned green. He swallowed convulsively. I thought he was going to throw up.

'Are —' He grabbed me by my left arm and twisted it up my back.

'Ow!' But he clapped his hand over my mouth.

'Be quiet!' he hissed. 'I don't know what game you're playing but I will hurt you if you don't do as I say.'

He manhandled me to the mouth of the alley. Still keeping a hold on me, John stuck his head out looking to the left and right, clutching me close to him. When he finally took me out, I saw various groups talking and laughing as they smoked in front of the club and across the road. But nobody looking our way.

I managed to get my teeth into the mound at the base of a finger and bit down hard. He yelped and pulled his hand away. I tried to call out for help but John yanked my arm further up and put his arm around my neck, turning our backs to the crowd so nobody could see.

I tried to resist but, with my arm twisted up behind me, I was on tiptoe, just trying to ease the pain as he walked me along the hoarding of the construction site. With his arm around my neck half-strangling me, his head bent to mine as if he were listening to me talk and my twisted arm out of sight between us, I suppose a casual look might show only an overly affectionate couple walking.

But nobody came near, no cars drove by in either direction.

The gate to the construction site was ajar, inside there was no one in sight. Even so, he took me through it cautiously, looking around him as we went. The guardhouse just inside was deserted, despite the lights inside being on. Elsewhere the site was dark.

Inside the gate, the ground was torn up and uneven with gouges and smashed concrete. John cursed as his foot slid in a muddy patch and his grip on me loosened. I twisted out of his grasp and scurried away, putting distance between us, glad of my running shoes, praying that I wouldn't trip and fall.

The rubble of a demolished building was still scattered across the lot in piles. I dodged between them as quietly as I could, zigzagging around them at random, trying to make my route difficult to follow. Where to hide? I couldn't hear John behind me. Was he sneaking up on me or just too far away? I chanced a quick look behind me but saw nothing.

I took a sharp right and dodged behind what seemed in the darkness like part of a broken wall. I needed a weapon to defend myself when he caught up. Quickly and as quietly as I could, I slipped The Bag over my head and emptied it on the ground. I hefted a couple of broken bricks and slipped one into The Bag and fastened the flap again.

Keeping The Bag on one shoulder, clutching it close to me, I peered across the site to see where the gate was. The lights at the gate seemed so far away but I had to get there. I plotted a path from pile to pile then, clutching The Bag to my chest, I braced myself and started out.

First pile. Stop. Look. Listen. Move.

Second pile. Stop. Look. Listen. Move.

Third pile. Almost there, just one more to go. Stop. Look.

'Gotcha!'

John caught my right shoulder, the one with The Bag, his hand was practically on the strap. I raised my elbow to knock his hand off and pivoted out of his grasp. Too bad I was too short for my elbow to get him in the face but I managed to get his hand off and stepped away, letting The Bag's strap slip down to sit around my right wrist.

'What is your problem?' I snapped, backing away from him.

He moved forward, closing the distance.

'Stay away from me! I don't want to hurt you!' All the while continuing to back away from him. He didn't look crazed but the very coolness of his expression was frightening. I let The Bag drop to the full length of its strap.

'I don't want to hurt you either. But it seems I have no choice. I can't let you tell —'

He reached for me and ...

'Oi!'

The cry came from the gate. John, distracted, looked towards it and I swung The Bag at him.

The Bag caught him on his arm. The brick inside was hard enough that he cried out, even as he kept reaching for me. I swung The Bag again, much higher, and this time I caught him on side of the head and he went down.

* * *

Turns out it was the night watchman who had yelled. He'd gone out to buy dinner and forgotten to lock the gate.

He let me use the phone in the guardhouse and I called 999 while he watched John. I'd left my address book in the little pile of belongings when I'd emptied my bag and at that particular moment I couldn't even remember my home number for love or money.

After hanging up, I guess I ran out of adrenaline. Knees shaky, cold sweat everywhere, I slid down and huddled on the floor to wait. Finally, it must have been minutes but felt like forever, I heard a car pull up outside the gate.

I dragged myself up and opened the gate to see a couple of young uniforms get out of a police patrol car and look around.

'Officers!' I called and waved to them.

'Miss! What happened?'

'Someone attacked me. The night watchman is guarding him over there.' I pointed them the right way and they picked their way over. I didn't follow.

Teck Wai and SIR showed up separately sometime later. SIR looked me up and down, pulled out his handphone and called for an ambulance.

'I'm okay! Really!'

He ignored me and went to join the young officers, Teck Wai trailing in his wake. A few words and the officers hurried back, one to me and the other to the patrol car. In short order, I was wrapped in a blanket and one officer was solicitously asking if I was hurt anywhere and for my parents' number while the other one carried the first aid kit over to where John was.

'Siao! You want my mother to have a heart attack, is it?

234

Police calling her at night about her daughter?' I spluttered. We finally agreed on him going to get me a hot sweet Milo while waiting for the ambulance to come.

SIR and Teck Wai walked John over. At least he could walk, albeit with supporting hands on both sides. He still looked a bit dazed but that didn't stop him from raising his handcuffed hands to point at me saying 'She's the one you should be arresting! She attacked me for no reason whatsoever!'

'What do you mean no reason? You asshole! You dragged me in here and said you were going to hurt me!'

'Take him to the car to wait for the ambulance,' SIR instructed the patrol officers. 'And call for another one.'

'I don't want an ambulance,' I said rather mulishly. 'I'm fine. I'm warm and I have a hot sweet drink, see?' I held up the steaming Styrofoam cup.

We went over the same ground about calling somebody to, presumably, comfort me? After all, I was an adult and did not need my mommy to look after me. Under SIR's quelling eye, I finally persuaded Teck Wai to let me call Shanti instead of my parents or Beng or Ling. After which call, I was given a choice of which car I would take to the police station. I picked SIR. I just needed some quiet time and figured it was more likely with him.

Bad luck for him because halfway there, I realised all my stuff, including my NRIC, house keys and pager, was still lying on the ground in the construction site and insisted he take me back there. It was not easy to find in the dark. Finally, with Krishnan's (I had finally asked what his name was) help, we did after something like half an hour.

SIR's eyebrows went up when I took the broken brick out of

The Bag and dumped in my stuff.

'I'm not sure if I should keep that brick for evidence,' he said but left it where it was.

Which means that Shanti made it to the HQ before I did. By the time I finally showed up, I had a very upset lawyer in the interview room. I could tell because, Miss Personal-Space-Please grabbed me, inspected me, shook me then almost hugged the life out of me.

'I'm okay! I'm okay! Put me down,' I gasped. Seeing my distress, SIR finally came to the rescue and calmed her down. When she finally let me go, I saw the tears standing in her eyes.

'I'm okay! I'm okay! Really!'

'You'd better be. What happened?'

SIR broke in, 'We were just about to ask her that very question. If we could move into the interview room —'

'If she needs legal representation —'

'No, no,' SIR soothed. 'We just want to find out what happened.'

'Inspector Rizwan, can she stay with me? Please?'

SIR wavered but, not waiting for an answer, Shanti went back into the interview room, sat in a chair and pulled me down into the chair next to hers.

Within minutes I was shivering, and Teck Wai had to go back out to get the blanket and wrap it around me. SIR went to the aircon controller and raised the temperature. Another cup of hot sweet Milo appeared. My hands appreciated the heat.

Teck Wai settled back at the table, opened his notebook and picked up his pen. So I started.

When I told them how John had reacted when I offered him

the Panda candy, SIR sat back in his chair and looked over at Teck Wai.

'The candy we found scattered around the dead girl.'

Teck Wai nodded. 'The MDMA.'

I looked at him confused and he clarified, 'Ecstasy.'

SIR looked back at me. 'Go on.'

'There isn't much more. He hauled me into the construction site, I got away, he chased me, I knocked him out.'

Teck Wai couldn't hold it in anymore. 'How?? You're so much smaller than he is!'

'Ya!' Shanti chimed in.

SIR snorted.

'I — uh — evened the odds with a brick.'

He frowned. I sighed.

'I had a brick in The Bag.'

Silence.

'You slammed him with a brick in The Bag?' Shanti made the connection.

'Twice!' I was starting to feel quite proud of myself.

'You could have killed him!' Teck Wai sounded appalled.

'He was going to kill me!' I thought a bit. 'Or at least hurt me.'

SIR coughed. 'Yes, please continue.'

'Uhh ... oh ya. Then Krishnan came and I asked him to guard John while I went to call the police. The police came, you came ... and that's it.'

I sat back in the chair, suddenly very tired. The clock on the wall said it was midnight, it already felt like I'd been awake all night. My eyelids were so heavy ...

'Inspectors, it's time to take Mei home.'

Home. I suddenly sat bolt upright! My parents! Would they be wondering where I was? I racked my unresponsive brain to remember what I'd told them. Dinner was all. I stood up.

'Yes, I have to get home.'

SIR nodded and looked to Teck Wai. 'Maybe get a patrol car?'

'If you don't mind, I'd like to drive her and Shanti back home. I'll come back after.'

SIR shrugged. 'Okay.'

Turning to me, he said, 'We'll type up your statement and you'll have to come back to sign it.'

I nodded, bouncing on the balls of my feet to keep awake.

Shanti rolled her eyes and put her arm around me to walk me out the door. 'Let's get you home.'

I don't remember much about the trip home. Shanti put me in the back seat and belted me in. Teck Wai said something but sleep, a black wave, came rushing in and I heard nothing until Shanti was shaking my shoulder and telling me to get out of the car.

The two of them walked me to the lift then up the flight of stairs to the flat. Turns out my parents were still awake, watching TV. Luckily Shanti was there to defuse their distress on seeing me being supported into the house by, not one, but two people.

'No, nothing major,' she told them. 'She's just very tired. It's okay, it's okay. I'll just put her to bed.'

Bed? Without a shower — I felt seriously icky — or brushing my teeth? That woke me up enough to insist that I was fine and that Teck Wai should take Shanti home.

The shower was everything I'd been wanting. I soaped myself from head to toe twice, each time rinsing off with hot water coursing over my head. That woke me up enough that I stayed awake long enough to brush my teeth.

Fending Ma off, I managed to get up into my bunk in the dark without waking Siew Ling, asleep in the lower bunk. Despite still feeling drained, adrenaline really takes it out of you, I lay wide awake for a while staring into the dark before climbing down again to switch on the table lamp. I finally fell asleep watching its mellow light over the edge of the bed.

29 Mar | Saturday

When I woke up this morning, the sun was streaming in the window. I sat bolt upright or tried to.

'Ow! Ow! Ow! Ow! Ow!'

Everything hurt. Flashes of last night came back to me. Asshole. I picked up my little alarm clock. Nine-thirty. Great. Now I was going to be late for work.

I slid down from my bed and padded out to the kitchen.

Ma was in there cooking chicken porridge. She turned as I came in.

'Wah! You're up. Breakfast is almost ready.'

'No time to eat.' I squeezed a bit of toothpaste on to my brush and stuck it in my mouth.

'Teck Wai didn't tell you? He said not to go to work today. He'll tell his mother.'

Brush still in mouth, I turned to stare at her. I quickly finished brushing my teeth, rinsed my mouth and splashed water on my face for good measure.

'What? Why?'

'He said to call him when you've had breakfast. He'll come take you to the police station.' She levelled a look at me. 'What were you doing last night, ah?'

I sighed. 'Long story. I tell you later, can?'

After a long hot shower that eased most of my aches and pains and getting dressed, which still involved a bit of moaning, I sat down to chicken porridge and coffee. Ma always cooks chicken porridge when we're sick. I guess recovering from being attacked counts as sick.

I told her what happened last night as I ate. She was silent for the most part although she did gasp when I told her how he dragged me into the construction site and nodded approvingly when I described slamming him with the brick in The Bag.

Just around that time, the phone rang and Ma waved me back down while she went to answer it.

'Hallo?'

'Ya. She's eating now. Almost finished.'

'Thirty minutes? Can.'

A click as she hung up and came back into the kitchen.

'Teck Wai coming in thirty minutes?' She nodded and I quickly ate the last spoonful of porridge and took my things to the sink to wash.

'Leave it, leave it,' Ma said so I went to wash out my mouth at the wash basin before checking The Bag. Both it and the stuff inside were dirty from their adventures in the construction site. Unfortunately I'd managed to dump my stuff in a muddy patch. I prodded the damp heap sadly. Some dry patches but mostly still damp. I dumped everything out on a spread newspaper outside the flat and started to clean.

It wasn't that much since everything that wasn't plastic or sealed in plastic was beyond redemption and had to be thrown. That pretty much left my wallet, keys, pager and water bottle. But The Bag was filthy and damp both inside and out.

What to do?

That's when Teck Wai showed up. He looked neat and clean, but, from the bruises under his eyes, I guessed he didn't get much sleep last night.

'What are you doing?'

'Ha! Everything's dirty from last night!' I answered as I picked up The Bag with my thumb and forefinger to show it to him before dropping it back on the newspaper.

'Don't you have another bag?' he asked.

I gave him a dirty look. 'No.'

'All you really need is your wallet and keys, right?' he persisted. 'Since I'll be bringing you back afterwards.'

I sighed and carried my stuff back into the flat. I spread The Bag out to dry in a corner, maybe I'd be able to brush off the mud before washing it, then took the other stuff into the kitchen. I rinsed the keys but could only wipe down the wallet before sticking it in my pocket. I wiped down the pager too but since I was coming straight back, I wouldn't need it so I left it on my table before going back out.

My running shoes were still muddy as well so I pulled my flip-flops from the shoe rack and joined Teck Wai outside as he was putting his shoes back on.

'Why am I going to the station again?' I asked.

'You need to confirm your statement. I spent this morning typing it up so you need to read it and sign it.'

'What if it's wrong?'

He gave me a long-suffering look and rolled his eyes. 'Then you have to correct it, of course!'

At the police station, I read through my statement and signed it. They had glossed over the brick in the bag but something was on my mind.

'So?' I asked. 'Did he kill Sally?'

Teck Wai, who was tapping the papers into a neat stack, stopped. 'Probably ... even though he says he didn't.'

'What? If he didn't, then who?'

'Donno lah! He probably did. He didn't say anything that you didn't mention, right?' He raised an eyebrow at me and I shook my head mutely.

'Anyway, even if he didn't kill Sally, he's already in big trouble. After you told us about his reaction to the Panda candy, we went to check his car and found a bag of Super Panda pills in his boot. Narcotics has a lot of questions to ask him.'

He snorted.

'Lucky for you we found the drugs. Otherwise maybe you kena time for grievous hurt. You managed to give him concussion, you know?'

'What was I supposed to do? Next time I get dragged into a construction site, just call you, is it?' I asked, aggrieved.

'Next time? Please lah! Can just stay out of trouble, can or not?'

Vomit blood.

'Are we done?' I asked icily.

He scanned the papers and nodded.

'Then I won't take any more of your time.'

I stood up and stalked out of the room and out of the station ignoring his calls to wait for him.

* * *

Police Cantonment Complex

By the time he'd gotten his papers together, she was out the main entrance and disappearing down the road. For somebody who'd been attacked last night, she was very fast. If she could walk that fast, there couldn't be much wrong with her. So hot tempered. He sighed and went back into the station.

After he handed Mei's signed statement to Inspector Rizwan, he sat at his desk and paged her ... but maybe she wouldn't call him back given how mad she was when she left.

He called her home number.

'Mei? I thought you were bringing her home?'

'Ah, she decided to go home on her own. Can ask her to call me back, please?'

He called Can-Do.

'Mei ah? I thought you told me she's not coming today?'

'I know ... If you see her can ask her to call me, please?'

'Ohh ... fight again, is it? Aiyo! The two of you aaa like small children li' dat.'

29 Mar | Saturday afternoon ... still

When I left Cantonment Complex, I was in a foul mood. Seriously! If somebody grabs you and drags you into a deserted construction site, you should be able to defend yourself without having to worry about being arrested. I mean, seriously!

I stomped onwards without a plan as I fumed. I didn't want to go home so I decided to go to work. After all, I was fine.

Unfortunately I didn't have my fare card, it being in the outside pocket of The Bag. I had to get off the first bus I boarded to go break a two-dollar bill for change. That did not make me any happier.

By the time I got to Holland Village, I'd calmed down a bit.

'Eh? How come you're here?' asked Auntie Fong when I showed up. 'Ah Wai called to —' She took in the scowl on my face at the mention of his name and broke off.

'Auntie Fong, if somebody grabs you and you hit them with a brick in a bag, is it your fault?'

'Of course not!' She did a double take. 'Someone grabbed you last night? Hai ya! That boy ah, he never said.'

I gave her the summary. I was already getting tired of telling the story.

'Aiyo! So the leng zai is a drug dealer, is it? Wasted!'

'Yaa …' I was starting to feel tired again. The anger that had carried me all the way here had worn off and my eyelids were drooping again.

'You need to sleep some more. Go home. Take taxi.' Her tone brooked no argument but my tummy had other ideas and spoke up good and loud. I groaned.

'Wah! So loud one, ah?' She laughed and gave my shoulder a little push. 'Go and eat something. Go!'

I went. What to eat, what to eat, what to eat? It was already past 2 pm and Ma would not be happy if I didn't eat dinner.

Imagine my surprise when Yock Li called to me when I stepped through the sliding doors. She was wearing a light short sleeved blouse with her jeans and her hair was pinned back with her pink clips. She looked even younger than her years … until you saw her eyes.

'I need to tell you something.'

'Now? Okay, if I can eat.' My stomach rumbled again and I rubbed it. 'Very hungry leh.'

Business at the mamak shop on Lorong Liput was slowing down after the lunch hour rush. Only a couple of tables were occupied so it was not a problem to find a table with no one nearby. I ordered a murtabak and two teh tariks and then joined Yock Li.

'What's up?'

'I … I need to warn you …'

'Ya …?' Her hair hung forward as she looked down and didn't say anything. I put my hand on hers.

'I heard about your arrest. Are you okay?'

Her head jerked up and she looked at me and suddenly tears were running down her cheeks. I got up, went around the table and put my arms around her. Her arms went around my waist and she held on with surprising strength. I patted her head. The server who brought my order looked at us askance but I just nodded for him to put it on the table and he did. I looked longingly at my hot crispy murtabak and my tummy rumbled again.

Yock Li who had her face pressed against it couldn't help but hear and feel that squidgy demand. She hiccupped a laugh and the sobs that had shaken her eased and soon she pulled her face away and released me.

As I went back to my seat, she sniffled and pulled a tissue from the packet she produced. Unable to wait any longer, I started to eat. The crispy roti layers parted with a crunch under my spoon as I pulled off a piece to dip in the spicy sour fish curry.

'I miss her. It was my fault. Everything was my fault.'

'Why was it your fault?'

She looked away from me then back again.

'I was the one who got her into selling Super Panda,' she choked. 'She needed the money and I thought that maybe if she joined me, she could earn the money without having to work so many hours.'

She looked down at her hands, twisting her damp tissue into a tight cord. Her teh tarik sat untouched. I was dying to ask her how she herself got into selling but I restrained myself. Given how upset she was, it would be better to just let her talk.

'She wanted to go to university. She wanted to get a good job so she could live on her own. She never wanted to ever see that man again! I thought it would fix everything!' Her hands closed into fists and the tissue cord snapped in two.

I chewed another mouthful thoughtfully and swallowed.

'So, what happened?'

'It went so well, at first.' She seemed to notice her cooling tea, picked it up and sipped. 'She did so well that she was taking more and more Super Panda to sell. And then that man overdosed. She got such a shock. We didn't know it was possible ...' Her hands tightened on the glass. 'Stupid, right? Not to know it was dangerous. It just looked like candy.'

'I'm not sure I would either.'

'After that, she said she didn't want to sell anymore.' She sighed and pushed away the glass. 'She came to get her money from me.'

'You were keeping her money?'

'Anything she wanted to keep away from that man, I would keep for her. He would go into her room and take anything he wanted.'

'That man means her father, is it?'

'Ya. That man.' Her contempt was profound. 'Too lazy to work but always wants money.'

'So, she came to get her money from you?'

'Ya. She flushed the pills down the toilet — she thought the police would come looking for her. She panicked. But she didn't have enough money to pay for the pills. I also didn't have.'

She stopped talking and picked up the scraps of tissue cord and twisted them together.

'So how?'

'She tried to borrow the money from her ex-boss but he only

gave her $100 … In the end, we couldn't get enough money to pay for the pills she flushed down the toilet.'

'Oh no …'

'So we bought lots of Panda candy. Super Panda looks a lot like Panda candy, you know.' She gave a bleak smile. 'Except Panda tastes good and Super Panda tastes horrible.

'In the ziplock bag, the Panda candy looked just like Super Panda. So we thought we could get away with it. Sally was going to tell Mr Kong she was quitting and give it to him. I went early and hid near where they were supposed to meet. I didn't know what I could do if he was angry but at least she wouldn't be there alone.

'He was smiling when he arrived. He is always smiling but when she told him she wanted to quit, he stopped smiling. I couldn't hear what she was saying — she was talking a long time. But I knew what she wanted to say. And then when she handed him the bag of Panda … He opened it!'

She sighed. 'I don't know why we didn't realise he would check. He grabbed her and next thing I knew he was holding her against the wall. I thought he was just making sure she didn't run away while he scolded her … I couldn't see properly. But when he let her go, she just fell down and lay there.'

She ignored my gasp. It was like she was talking to herself, not me.

'I waited for a while after he left. Then I went to Sally. Her eyes were open but her face … when I called her, she didn't move. All I could smell was shit and Panda.'

She gulped and stopped. I thought she was going to throw up. I thought I was going to throw up and pushed my murtabak away half-eaten. Yock Li sat lost in a world of her own. Reliving the experience? I reached out and put my hand over hers. She started and looked at me, eyes wide and pain-filled.

'I couldn't stand to look at her like that. So I just closed her eyes and left.' Tears welled and she gripped my hand hard. 'I just left her there, Mei.'

I patted her hand with my free one. 'There's nothing you could have done for her.'

'That's why you have to stay away from Mr Kong!' Yock Li burst out. 'He killed Sally! He might hurt you too.'

'Yes, I get that. But you also need to tell the police what you saw.'

'I'm scared,' she whispered.

'They already know about the Super Panda so there's no need to be scared. You'll be helping them, right?' I said briskly.

'Can come with me?' She looked pleadingly at me.

'Can!'

* * *

We were halfway across the carpark when we heard footsteps running up behind us. I turned just in time to get the full weight of Chloe barrelling into me. I went down and got a good crack on my head, which knocked me out for a moment.

When I came to she had disappeared but I could hear yelling. I sat up gingerly touching the back of my head and found Yock Li and Chloe scuffling on the ground. Yock Li seemed to be getting the worst of it. I groaned to my feet and pitched in, catching Chloe by the neck and hauling her back. Suddenly strangled,

Chloe released Yock Li who rolled to her feet and launched herself at Chloe.

I managed to get out of the way just in time as Chloe went down on her back. Yock Li sat on her chest and started to slap her. She got in two before I managed to stop her. Tears were streaming down her cheeks as she panted.

'She tried to kill you!' she cried as I restrained her

'Why are you with her?' wailed Chloe. 'First it was Sally and now that she's gone, it's her! Why not me? It's never me!' Looking at me venomously, she spat, 'Why didn't you just fall on the track and die?'

'That was you who pushed me?'

'You little —' she started to struggle out from under Yock Li and we both moved to pin her.

It wasn't very easy with her screaming and struggling but an uncle came running over to help. Eventually we managed to get her up and walking even as we restrained her. It took us over half an hour to get her to the Buona Vista Police Post, normally a five- to ten-minute walk. She struggled and screamed all the way. People we passed stared at us. With us walking behind the uncle who led the way, it was a strange procession.

The young police officers manning the reception were somewhat taken aback at the sight of us. Yock Li and I were fully occupied because Chloe was struggling even harder so the uncle ended up having to tell them what happened.

'I just pulled into the carpark,' he said, 'and saw the two girls just walking when that one in the middle came running, pushed the small one down and was going to bang her head on the road again when that one with the pink hairclips pulled her off. I had to park my car properly so I didn't see what happened after that but when I finally got there the two of them were trying to get her up. And then we walked here.'

He had a car? Wouldn't it have been faster to bring us here by car instead of having to restrain Chloe as we walked? On the other hand, he did come with us so I couldn't really complain, at least we had a witness on hand. Given we'd been rolling on the ground, he probably didn't want to have us dirty his back seat.

One of the policemen came out and we let go of her. It looked like she was about to run but he took her firmly by the arm and led her into a small room off the reception area.

Once she was gone, Yock Li and I slumped into the chairs and caught our breath. A young officer, his name tag said 'Tan Kok Boon', came to us with clipboards and pens. As I accepted a set, before he walked away, I caught his wrist and whispered to him.

'Could you please call Inspector Chan Teck Wai? Or Station Inspector Rizwan? And ask them to come here?'

'What?' he asked, startled. 'Why?'

'We need to talk to them urgently. Tell him that Mei and Yock Li need to talk to him urgently.'

'But —'

'Please! I can give you Teck Wai's handphone number.' I tore off a piece of the form and hastily scribbled it down for him.

'Oh … okay.' He still looked doubtful but when he went back to his desk, I saw him pick up the phone and dial.

I heaved a sigh of relief then started inspecting my various grazes. I winced when I touched the back of my head. There was a massive bump and my hair was gritty. Uncle Lee, as he told us to call him, who was sitting behind me asked, 'You okay or not?'

'I'm okay, I'm okay.'

'She banged her head very hard when Chloe knocked her over.' Yock Li put in anxiously. 'I heard it.'

Uncle Lee went over to Officer Tan but he was still on the phone and so he spoke to the other young policeman instead. They both came over to me and I said mutinously 'I'm fine. I just have a bump on my head.'

Nevertheless, Police Officer Rajesh Sivalingam insisted on taking a look at the bump and then to clean it. Then I had to fill out the form.

Uncle Lee handed in his clipboard and started to fuss about needing to pick his wife up and how angry she was going to be at his non-appearance so they let him go. We thanked him and said our goodbyes before returning to our clipboards.

And the next thing I knew, both Teck Wai and SIR were walking in.

I tried to stand up but Yock Li clung to me.

'It's okay,' I told her comfortingly and squeezed her hand. She nodded and stood up with me. SIR gave her a quizzical look then turned to me enquiringly.

'We have something to tell you.'

29 Mar | Saturday evening

It took quite a while to prepare for interrogation.

Although the police brought in a pleasant-looking older woman whom they referred to as an 'appropriate adult' to accompany her during the interrogation, Yock Li insisted that I stay with her as well. Teck Wai wasn't happy but SIR agreed readily enough.

I had to call Ma to tell her I wouldn't be home for dinner. She was not happy when she heard I was in a police station again. I hastily assured her that Teck Wai would be bringing me home and hung up.

* * *

We sat at the table, the appropriate adult to one side of Yock Li, me on the other. It seems they had to rearrange one of their activity rooms to accommodate the number of people sitting in on the interrogation. Besides Yock Li's team of three, facing us was SIR, Teck Wai, a hard-faced man from the Narcotics Division as well as a sergeant from the Buona Vista station itself.

Nervous with all those people looking at her, Yock Li's hand tightened on mine. I squeezed it back. She wasn't alone.

SIR started off gently, asking her if she was comfortable, did she want a hot drink, was the aircon too cold. Once she relaxed, her answers coming naturally, he got to the point; matter-of-factly asking her to tell him her story from the beginning.

'I was going to clubs since I was in Sec 3. Just for fun, you know,' she started. 'Then one night, I met Mr Kong there. I was so scared. I thought he would scold me or tell my parents. But he didn't; he just smiled and waved like we were just friends. I started to see him regularly. Sometimes we would arrange to meet up — he'd buy me drinks and snacks. Then one night he asked me if I wanted to make some extra pocket money. And that's how it started.'

As Yock Li told her story, SIR would ask her questions, taking her back and forth, garnering more information each time. Teck Wai and the Narcotics Division officer took copious notes, even with the tape recorder on the table capturing every word that was said.

Earning money had just been an added perk for Yock Li, her parents were generous with her pocket money. Pretty, bubbly and outgoing, she was a natural at sales. The excitement and achievement were what drove her. And pleasing him. I got the feeling that she had been infatuated with John and would have agreed to anything he asked.

Happy as she was, she didn't notice that Sally was having problems until she found her cleaning tables in the canteen. Yock Li cornered her and made her tell her what was going on. Sally had cried in her arms, exhausted from working to earn enough to support herself while still trying to keep her grades up. She wanted to get a university degree, get a good job and never see her father again.

Yock Li had tried to give her money but Sally had refused, only accepting a loan because her father had taken the money she needed to pay her school fees. She was going to start a new job in a karaoke lounge that paid better. Hopeful that with the tips, she would earn enough to be able to work fewer hours.

It didn't work out. Sally, too young and inexperienced, couldn't connect with the old men out to drink and enjoy the company of women. Unable to flirt and charm them into spending money. The owner was not happy; Sally was sure that he was going to fire her.

Eager to help her best friend, Yock Li persuaded John to let Sally join her in the business of selling Super Panda. She promised that she would train her and that Sally would do a good job.

And she did. With some investment in a trendy, flattering haircut and suitable clothes for dancing (all chosen by Yock Li), she was an attractive girl and, with some coaching, able to flirt with the club crowd and make her sales targets.

'She was so happy,' Yock Li said. 'She was making enough money to live on and even save for uni and still had time to study.'

Soon, Sally was increasing her sales targets. She needed the money, she was motivated. Her savings were growing nicely.

'And then that man took everything.'

Sally couldn't open a savings account without Jimmy knowing. So she had been hiding her savings around the house, leaving small easy-to-find caches to keep Jimmy happy. And that had worked until she came home one night to find her room torn apart and all her savings gone.

'Sally was so upset but I said "Don't worry lah! You can make more quite easily now."'

And that's when Yock Li started keeping Sally's money for her.

And everything was going well until Chinese New Year. All the ang mohs left town, taking advantage of the two-day holiday. All the Chinese were tied up with family celebrations. As a result, Sally's customer base was seriously reduced. She had too much Super Panda on her hands and no takers.

Then a repeat customer at the club turned out to live in a neighbouring block. Recognizing Sally, he had asked her to sell him a few pills. They met in the void deck of her block for the transaction.

Eager for the buzz, he popped all the pills at the same time. He made a face then asked her to go buy him a drink to get the taste out of his mouth; she could buy herself one as well. He gave her the money and she went off to the coffee shop. It was quite busy and it took a while for her to get the drinks.

When she got back to the void deck, she found him convulsing on the floor. She tried to restrain him but he was too strong and she rushed off to the payphone to call 995.

'She was so scared. We didn't know that Super Panda could do that,' Yock Li said.

On hanging up, she realised that once the authorities knew it was drugs, they would go looking for it. If she still had the pills, they would find out that she was the one who sold it to him.

She rushed home and flushed the rest of the pills down the toilet.

But once the pills were gone, her panic faded and she realised she had another problem. How was she going to pay for them? It was one thing if she had returned the unsold pills but without them? Did she have enough money to pay for them?

'She was pressing the doorbell and knocking the door like mad. When Maizura, our maid, opened the door, Sally was sweating like anything and so white I thought she was sick. I was going to ask her to see doctor but she immediately dragged me to my room and locked the door.'

Sally told Yock Li what happened and that she wanted to stop selling Super Panda.

'She said that even though the money was good — what if someone else died?'

The two girls got to work and counted Sally's savings. She owed John about $28,000 for the supply she'd gotten from him but, all in all, she only had around $5,509. Where was she going to get the rest of the money to pay him? She had to pay him the following Saturday.

Yock Li wasn't earning as much as Sally and she wasn't really saving so she only had about $3,000. They were still short $20,000.

In the following week, the two girls did their best to get together the rest of the money but they failed. Desperate, Sally went to see Uncle Seng but even he didn't have the money, or so he said. He'd given her $100 but that was nowhere near how much she needed.

Finally, Sally said that she would just give Mr Kong what money she had and tell him what happened — hopefully he would understand why she didn't want to sell Super Panda anymore. He was kind and surely he would give her time to pay back the rest of the money.

But that would leave her in a bad position; it would be difficult to earn the remaining money with normal part-time jobs. Yock Li had the idea to buy Panda candy and give it to him instead, telling him it was the remainder of the Super Panda. He wouldn't be able to tell.

'Sally didn't think it would work but I told her that worst come to worst, she could just say sorry and tell him that she would pay him the rest as she earned,' Yock Li said. 'It's not so easy to earn $20k leh … she was even talking about going to work in Geylang. Last time, she could barely make enough to eat; how to earn $20k to pay back?'

That night, Yock Li went with Sally to the club. Sally needed her support, she was in a terrible state, pale, sweating and so nervous she kept wanting to throw up. She went into the club to use the toilet, the nearest one available. They agreed to meet at the bus stop after Sally's appointment with Mr Kong.

'I knew where he was meeting her, so I went to find a place to hide so I could see.'

Sally was to meet Mr Kong in the alley between Zouk and the construction site. Far in enough that they could see anybody coming in. At the other end there was a clump of trees by the river.

'I didn't want him to see me so I was hiding behind a tree, quite far in, just near enough to see.'

Even though the alley was dark, she could see Sally waiting, and then Mr Kong arrived. Although she could see them, albeit not very clearly, she couldn't hear them — they were talking in whispers.

She saw Sally hand him the Panda package — they had wrapped it in a white supermarket plastic bag. He took out the zip-lock bag and looked at it. Suddenly, he grabbed Sally and slammed her up against the wall and kept her there for a long time. Yock Li couldn't see what was happening; he had his back to her. But when he finally released Sally, she fell to the ground. He stooped to pick something up. Then he walked away.

'I waited for a while to make sure he was gone then I went to her.' Yock Li choked and covered her face with her hands. I put my arms around her and she leaned against me shaking. Teck Wai frowned but I ignored him.

After a while, she sat up straight again and the appropriate adult passed her a packet of tissues.

While I listened to her telling them about finding Sally dead, I found myself wondering why John had killed her. Was it because of the Panda substitution or was it because she had decided to stop peddling Super Panda? If he was hot-tempered, maybe the former. I thought about how he grabbed me last night.

Was it only just last night? It felt like a month ago.

Was that the action of a hot-tempered man? Or a cold-blooded, decisive man of action.

Yock Li was terrified that Mr Kong would know that she had been there; would he kill her too? She went into the club and stayed in the toilet as long as she could before she had to go home.

The next day when he asked her where Sally was, saying that she hadn't shown up at their appointment, Yock Li told her that she didn't know, she hadn't seen Sally recently.

She had to continue selling Super Panda in the clubs in case he came to check. She had to behave as normally as she could; she couldn't afford to have someone comment that she was behaving strangely until the announcement of Sally's death. Only then could she break down and let out the tears that she'd been holding in.

When Lakshmi passed her the photo of Sally and her, she had cried again. Chloe started yelling at Lakshmi and it had escalated until a teacher had intervened. Unfortunately, the furore had drawn Mr Kong's attention. He had paged her and, when she responded, asked her what happened. When she told him about the photograph, he told her to find out where it came from; maybe it was related to Sally's murder.

'He acted all angry and upset about it,' Yock Li said. 'He didn't know that I was there and actually saw him kill her.'

Finding out from Lakshmi that she had gotten the photograph from me, Yock Li went to see her and found out about Sally's letter to her mother. When she reported to Mr Kong as instructed, he just thanked her.

She didn't think any more about it until Chloe told her that she had seen Mr Kong walking out with me a couple of times, speculating that he was interested in me. However, Yock Li didn't think his reasons were romantic and went to the bookshop to warn me. Unfortunately, when she was actually talking to me, she realised she didn't know how to do so without telling me everything. So she left without saying anything.

When SIR asked her why she didn't tell them all this when she was arrested, she looked at him like she thought he was stupid. She hadn't thought they would believe her and she was afraid that if Mr Kong found out that she had told them he would kill her like he killed Sally.

So, what made her decide to tell me? SIR wanted to know.

She looked at me then back at SIR. 'I had to warn her. What if he tries to kill her? Like he killed Sally?' Her eyes filled with tears and she put her hand across her mouth, stifling her sobs.

I put my arms around her and crooned, 'It's okay, it's okay … I'm okay.' She leaned her head against mine, eyes closed, shaking.

SIR said, 'Then you'll be happy to know that we arrested Mr Kong last night.'

Her head came up sharply, eyes wide, tears wet on her cheeks.

'H-how? Why?'

SIR indicated me with a nod. 'He attacked her.'

I heard the appropriate adult gasp and the NarcO actually stopped writing for a moment and looked up in surprise. Yock Li stared at me in disbelief. I nodded.

'How come … how did you escape?'

I shrugged uncomfortably. 'I hit him with The Bag.'

And then when she continued to gape, I added, 'There was a brick in it.'

Teck Wai rolled his eyes but the NarcO's eyes rounded in approval and he looked at me consideringly.

SIR went on, 'So far he's being charged with assault and possession of controlled drugs; we found Super Panda in the boot of his car. We already knew that he was involved in the death of Sally Song but with your help, I think that we will be adding to the present charges.'

'Really?' Yock Li cried and then she burst into tears. Again. But this time they were tears of relief.

* * *

Finally, we were done. It was almost 9 pm. Teck Wai told me to wait outside while he finished up inside.

So I waited in reception with Yock Li until her parents came to take her home. From the looks on their faces, she was going to have a lot of explaining to do. She hugged me convulsively and I gave her my pager number before she left.

Chloe's parents, however, were still talking to the police. I'd included her attempt to push me onto the MRT tracks when I filled in the complaint form. That made two attacks. She has issues.

When Teck Wai and I finally left, he first took me to NUH Emergency to get my head checked. After triage, we had to wait to see the doctor. It felt like forever, but I think it was only an hour. Any nausea I had was gone and I was hungry enough to insist that he buy me a lapful of snacks while we waited.

When I finally saw the doctor, Teck Wai insisted on going in with me! As though I were five years old. I reluctantly admitted to having been knocked out when my head hit the ground but since it was hours ago and I was showing no signs of concussion, she said I could go home but was to come back if I felt worse.

* * *

National University Hospital Carpark

By the time they reached his car, Teck Wai could tell that Mei wasn't going to be awake much longer. She managed to get into the car and belt herself in but by the time he got into the driver's seat, she was asleep.

He looked at her for a long moment.

She was so tiny that he'd always discounted her as a child; he still couldn't believe that she had fought off a man a good 30 cm taller than she was. Was it just luck? Even if it was, he was still impressed.

She had even managed to get the girl to talk to them after being attacked twice in two consecutive days. With Yock Li now willing to talk, it would be much easier to make the case against John Kong for the death of Sally Song. And Narcotics would be eager to talk to her for their case too.

He put the car into gear and pulled out of the parking lot. Maybe he'd buy her dinner some time.

Epilogue

'Yaaaaammmmm SENG!' echoed through the restaurant for the third time.

And everybody downed their drinks of choice then sat again to continue eating. Alex, bespectacled and beaming, and Ling, radiant in her red and gold cheongsam began to do their tour of the tables. I accompanied them as part of their entourage, carrying a bottle of VSOP to top up their glasses.

Actually, Alex doesn't have a head for alcohol so we had decanted the actual brandy and filled it with strong oolong tea so that the whole entourage could toss back their drinks in grand style.

Auntie Fong was sitting at the fifth table we visited. After the table had toasted the couple and taken the requisite photo with the bride and groom, I hung back a bit to greet her.

'Wah, you look so pretty tonight!' Auntie Fong exclaimed. 'Your cheongsam is new, is it?'

'Ya, my mother had it tailor-made. Nice, right?'

I was very pleased with it. I loved the warm brown satin with dull gold chrysanthemums and it had a bit of stretch, allowing it to fit closely without constricting.

'Turn, turn! Let me see properly.'

So I put down my bottle and vogued for her, twisting and

posing in imitation of the magazine models … until I looked over my shoulder to find Teck Wai watching me. He was leaning on the back of his mother's chair, smiling amusedly.

Aiyo… so embarrassing! I could feel the heat in my cheeks spread all the way to my ears. Quickly distract!

'Wah, Inspector Chan! I didn't expect to see you,' I said as nonchalantly as I could manage. 'No bad guys to chase today, is it?'

'Ya lah! Since you're here and not out there causing trouble …' he said, lips quirking as I wrinkled my nose at him before turning to check where the entourage was. They were just done with the next table and moving on.

'Eeks! I better catch up with Ling and Alex,' I said hurriedly, picking up the VSOP bottle and hurrying to catch up with the entourage.

The hairs on the back of my neck prickled and I took a quick look back to see both Auntie Fong and Teck Wai turning to see the server place a steamed fish on the lazy Susan.

I really want to know how I got home after he took me to Emergency. Or maybe I don't. The last thing I remember was getting into his car. After that, nothing. Did he sleepwalk me back to the flat? I hope so. Because the alternative was that he carried me up. That did not bear thinking about.

I got to Alex and Ling and the rest of the entourage in time to refill their glasses. Everybody at the table stood and picked up their drinks.

The entourage bawled, 'Long life and happiness to the bride and groom!'

'YAMMMMMMMMMMMMMMMMMMMMM SENG!'

Glossary

Singlish has been variously described as a form of colloquial English, pidgin English, a creole language or a patchwork patois of local languages, but more than anything I think of it as the sound of Singapore, with its own special rhythms,

Like all living languages, Singlish evolves constantly and the vocabulary and references used today differ slightly from my youth. This being the case, some of the Singlish terms I use in this book may be unfamiliar even to Singaporeans born in the 21st century so I have included definitions of as many of them as I can.

Ah Gong	Grandfather (Teochew).
Ah Gu	Maternal uncle (Teochew).
ABC	Air Batu Campur (Malay) aka ice kacang (Malay). See 'Ice kacang'.
Act blur	To play innocent, ignorant or confused. See 'Blur'.
Ai mai	Want [or] don't want (Hokkien). Can also mean 'Should I, shouldn't I'
Ang moh	Red hair (Hokkien). Probably referred originally to the Dutch. Now refers to Caucasian people in general.

Asam pedas fish	More correctly "ikan asam pedas". A classic Malay and Minangkabau dish, it is sour spicy fish stew.
Asam laksa	Laksa is a spicy noodle soup. Unlike the coconut-based Singapore laksa, the asam laksa from Penang has a sour fish soup base and lots of shredded cucumber and pineapple pieces.
Atas	Above (literal, Malay). Means 'high class'.
Beehoon goreng putih	White fried rice vermicelli (Malay).
Belinjo chips	A popular deep fried crispy snack made from the seeds of the belinjo or melinjo tree. It has a savoury bitter flavour which is addictive.
Blur	Confused or slow to catch on.
Boh eng	No time (Hokkien).
Boh hew	Don't care (Hokkien).
Boh pian	No choice (Hokkien).
Bù shì	It's not right (Mandarin).
Buat bodoh	Play stupid (literal, Malay). Act like you don't know.
Buay tahan	Cannot take it (Hokkien).
Buy back	Abbreviation of 'buy and bring back' (Singlish).
Cabut	Leave (Malay).
CBD	Central Business District.
COE	Certificate of Entitlement. Before you can register a vehicle, you must first bid for a COE. This represents the right to vehicle ownership for ten years. The COE system started in 1990 and is an integral part of the Vehicle Quota

	System which regulates the vehicle population in Singapore, which is one of the densest in the world.
Char bor	Girl (Hokkien).
Char kuay teow	Dry fried flat rice noodles. The recipe varies from place to place.
Chau	Gone (Hokkien).
Chau liao	Already gone (Hokkien).
Chendol	A dessert that comprises coconut milk, palm sugar syrup, short green rice flour noodles scented with pandan and shaved ice. Commonly found in Southeast Asia.
Chochoking	Teasing, provoking. From the Malay word 'cucuk' which means to prick or poke.
Chope	Reserve (Singlish). Originally a call for a pause or retraction when playing games.
Chup	Mixed (Cantonese).
Desker	Desker Road is known for its transvestite and trans-sexual prostitutes.
Die	Short for 'going to die'. Often used as an expression of dismay at impending disaster.
Die die must try	A popular phrase when talking about food. It means that you have got to try it even if you die in the process.
Don't play play	Don't mess around. See 'main-main'.
Duck eggs	Local slang for 'zero'.
Dulang	Tray (Malay).
Durian runtuh	Fallen durian (literal, Malay). Means 'windfall'.
Eh sai boh	'Can or not?' (Hokkien).

ELDDS	English Literature, Drama and Debating Society.
ECA	Extra-curricular activities.
Five-foot-way	A roofed, continuous walkway commonly found in front of shophouses in Malaysia, Singapore and Indonesia. Supposed to be 5 feet in width (origin of the name) but may be narrower or wider.
Fong sup	Pain attributed to wind and dampness entering the body usually from constant contact with water, especially from the habit of bathing after sunset … or in this case, sleeping in an air-conditioned room.
Fren fren	Friendly or more specifically platonically friendly.
Gahmen	Local slang for Government.
Garang	Fierce (Malay).
Gatal	Itching (literal, Malay). Looking for trouble.
Geylang	The area now named 'Geylang' was originally an Orang Laut settlement called 'Geylang Kelapa' which was a coconut plantation. It is suggested that 'geylang' is a corruption of 'kilang', the Malay word for 'factory' referring to the presses and mills used to squeeze oil from the copra. Geylang is home to dozens of temples as well as a red-light district and is a popular destination for those in search of supper and durians.

Goondu	Idiot. Apparently originates from the Tamil word for 'fat' or 'round'.
Gula melaka	Palm sugar (Malay).
HDB	The Housing Development Board is the statutory board under the Ministry of National Development which is responsible for Singapore's public housing.
Hae ko	Prawn paste (Hokkien).
Hai yah	Exclamation denoting exasperation. May also be spelled 'hai ya'.
Ho seh	Hokkien exclamation of satisfaction.
Hokkien	The largest Chinese dialect group in Singapore. The Hokkiens in Singapore come mainly from Zhangzhou and Quanzhou, two prefectures in Fujian province, China.
Hong bao	Red packet (Hokkien). Money given by married folk to the unmarried folk during the Chinese New Year.
Hungry Ghost	Refers to Hungry Ghost month when, by tradition, the gates of Hell are opened, releasing spirits to roam the earth. It is the seventh month in the Chinese calendar. The actual Hungry Ghost Festival falls on the 15th night but festivities go on all month.
Ice kacang	Ice or ais kacang is a popular local dessert with shaved ice covering such treats as sweet red bean, cubes of grass jelly, sweet corn. Multicoloured syrups and evaporated milk

are drizzled over it. Add-ons like fresh mango and durian are popular.

Ikan bilis	Dried anchovy (Malay).
Jaga	Watch, look after (Malay).
Jalan	This Malay word has many meanings including road, way, route. 'Jalan kaki' means to walk.
Jalan-jalan	To go for a walk (Malay).
Jangan	Do not (Malay).
Jiak	Eat (Hokkien).
Jiak hong	Literally means 'eat wind' (Hokkien), a direct translation of the Malay term 'makan angin' which means to go on holiday.
Jiak zua	Literally means 'Eat snake' (Hokkien). Refers to the act of skiving.
Jialat	To sap one's energy (Hokkien). Arduous, troublesome.
Jiě jie	Mandarin for elder sister (姐姐).
Jin ho jiak	Very tasty (Hokkien).
Kacau-kacau	Stir up trouble. 'Kacau' means 'disturb' (literal, Malay).
Kaki	Close friend or buddy. Likely an abbreviation of 'kaki lang' (自家人) which means 'my own people' in Hokkien.
Kan cheong	Nervous or excited (Hokkien).
Kangkong	A semi-aquatic vegetable. It has a variety of names in English, including water spinach, river spinach, water convolvulus and water morning glory.

Kang kor	Troublesome, uncomfortable (Hokkien).
Kaypoh verb	Nosy or busy body. Can be used as a noun, and adjective.
Kena	Being on the receiving end of something (Malay). Generally that something is unpleasant. For example, 'kena sai' means 'get hit by shit'.
Kena tekan	Get pressed (literal, Malay). Means to be under pressure, oppressed or bullied.
Kiā kiā	'Kiā' means 'scared' (Hokkien). 'Kiā kiā' means 'jumpy' or 'nervous'.
Kiam chai	Actually means salted (preserved) vegetable (Hokkien/Teochew). To 'look like kiam chai' means to look messy and crumpled.
Kiam siap	Stingy (Hokkien).
Kong si mi?	What are you saying? (Hokkien).
Kopi	Local-style coffee. For authentic kopi, Robusta coffee beans are roasted with margarine and sugar at high heat. The ground coffee is brewed with hot water and strained through a cotton sock filter. The standard kopi is served with condensed milk already added.
Kopi gao siu dai	Stronger coffee with less condensed milk.
Kreta Ayer	Kreta Ayer Complex (牛车水大厦) is the old name for Chinatown Complex.
Kuching kurap	Mangy cat (literal, Malay). Means small or insignificant.

Kueh pie tee	A popular Peranakan dish which comprises a small crispy deep-fried case that you fill with a variety of ingredients just before you pop it into your mouth.
Lau lang	Old people (Hokkien).
Lai jiak	Come eat (Hokkien/Teochew).
Leh chey	Troublesome. Originated from 'leceh' (Malay).
Leng zai	Handsome boy (Cantonese).
Lou po	Wife (Cantonese).
M&B	Mills and Boons. A popular publisher of romance novels.
MacRitchie	Refers to MacRitchie Reservoir Park, part of Singapore's Central Catchment Nature Reserve.
Maggi mee	A brand of instant noodles. Possibly the first in Southeast Asia.
Main-main	Fooling or messing around (Malay). This phrase was the origin of the Singlish 'play play'.
Mak	Abbreviation of 'emak' which means 'mother' (Malay).
Makan	Eat (Malay).
Mamak	Refers to a Tamil Muslim living in Singapore or Malaysia. Originates from the Tamil word 'māmā' which means 'maternal uncle'.
Mèi mei	Mandarin for 'younger sister' (妹妹).
Mm tzai si	Ignorant of death (Hokkien). Reckless.
Minangkabau	The largest ethnic group on the island of Sumatera, Indonesia.
Mugger	One who studies hard, studious. (Singlish).
Mugging	Studying hard. (Singlish).

Mulut gatal	Itchy mouth (Literal, Malay). Means to want a snack.
Murtabak	Filled prata eaten with curry. The filling usually contains minced mutton or chicken and egg.
Nasi padang variety	Minangkabau steamed rice served with a variety of pre-cooked dishes. It is named after the city of Padang in West Sumatera.
NIE	National Institute of Education.
NRIC	National Registration Identity Card.
NUS	National University of Singapore.
Ngiao	Fussy, picky (Hokkien).
Ngoh hiang	Teochew-style five spice pork rolls. Minced meat is seasoned and mixed with chopped crunchy yam bean (jicama) or water chestnuts, wrapped with beancurd skin and deep fried. Usually sliced into pieces before serving.
Niang dou fu	Originally a Hakka dish, it now comprises a range of fresh and fried items such as vegetables and bean curd items stuffed with fish paste or minced meat. May be served dry or in soup or laksa gravy with noodles or rice.
Oi	Exclamation equivalent to 'Hey!'.
Orh-nee	Teochew yam paste dessert with a lot of lard and sugar. Not for those trying to lose weight.
Otak-otak	Penang-style 'otak-otak' is a delicious dish of spicy fish custard with daun kadok (wild pepper) steamed in a banana leaf package.

Pad kra pao	Chicken stirfried with Thai basil and served hot on rice, generally with a fried egg. (Thai)
Pad thai	Stirfried rice noodles with meat, seafood or tofu, eggs and vegetables and garnished with peanuts. Authentically accompanied by containers of chilli powder, sugar and fish sauce that you add to taste. (Thai)
Pai kia	Bad boy (Hokkien).
Pak tor	To go out on a date (Hokkien).
Pakcik	Uncle (Malay). Used as a term of respect. See 'Uncle'.
Panas	Hot (Malay).
Pek kim	White gold (literal, Hokkien). Money given to the deceased's family at a funeral.
Pok kai	Originates from 'puk gaai' (Cantonese) which literally means 'to fall into the street'. Means 'to go broke'.
Poly	Abbreviation of 'polytechnic'.
Prata	An Indian fried bread. The dough is stretched out until thin and then folded to form layers before it is fried. Served with curry. A very popular breakfast or snack.
Pucat	Pale (Malay).
Rojak	A Southeast Asian salad usually of fruit and vegetables. The most basic Penang or fruit rojak usually comprises pieces of cucumber, pineapple and jicama. These are tossed in rojak sauce together with coarse ground peanuts. The Penang rojak sauce contains black prawn paste,

	thick black soya sauce among other things.
Sai	Shit (Hokkien).
Sai mun chai	Mosquitoes (literal, Cantonese). Grandchildren.
Sambal	A Malay/Indonesian condiment comprising chilli ground with shallots, shrimp paste and other herbs.
Sarong party girl	A local party girl who targets foreign men. She may not be a girl.
Sayang	A Malay word that has many meanings, in the context used here, it's an endearment.
Sek	Eat (Cantonese).
Sek zor mei	Have you eaten? (Cantonese).
Shiok	Very enjoyable. Origins unclear but widely used in Malaysia and Singapore.
Si mi tai ji	What's the problem? (Hokkien).
Siao	Crazy (Hokkien).
Siao char bor	Crazy girl (Hokkien).
Siong	Difficult (Hokkien).
Soto ayam	Malay or Indonesian chicken soup served with cubes of pressed rice. The soup is spiced with fresh turmeric, herbs and other spices like cumin and coriander.
Sotong	Squid in this context (Malay). Also refers to cuttlefish and octopus.
Suka-suka	As you like (Malay).
Sup tulang merah	Red bone soup (literal, Malay). Refers to a thick red stew of mutton bones where the piece de resistance is the marrow which you suck, scoop, however you can get it out of the

	cracked bones. Messy to eat but oh so good!
Tahan	Withstand (Malay).
Taukwa	Firm tofu.
Teh halia	Ginger tea (literal, Malay). Refers to Indian style tea with ginger served with condensed milk added.
Teh-O kosong	Black tea without milk or sugar.
Teh tarik	Pulled tea (literal, Malay). Indian style aerated tea served with condensed milk added. The tea is aerated by pouring it from one container to another ('pulled') resulting in a foamy beverage. This is an art in itself as the further apart the two containers are the better the aeration.
Teochew	The second largest Chinese dialect group in Singapore. The Teochew people originated in the Chaoshan region in eastern Guangdong, China.
Teochew moi	Teochew-style rice porridge, watery with grains that are still distinct unlike the Cantonese style.
Tolong	Please or help (Malay).
Tofu	Soya bean curd.
Tom yum goong	A hot and sour Thai soup with prawns. (Thai)
Tong shui	Traditional Chinese desserts.
Too-thor th'ng	A peppery pig's stomach soup which is a common dish in some Peranakan Chinese homes.
Tua chiak	Big one (Hokkien).
Tudung	Cover (literal, Malay). Also refers to the

	headcovering worn by some Muslim women.
Tulang	Bone (Malay). Used here as an abbreviation for 'Sup Tulang Merah'.
Uncle	A term of respect used when addressing an older man. Also used as a term referring to an older man.
Void deck	Refers to the ground floor of HDB blocks which have been left open as a sheltered space for the residents' use.
Vomit blood	Comes from the Hokkien phrase, 'tor hwee' (吐血). Refers to the feeling of extreme frustration or aggravation. May be making reference to bleeding ulcers.
Wah	Exclamation of amazement or surprise.
Wah lau	The most commonly used polite version of the Hokkien phrase 'wah lan', which loosely translates to 'oh penis'. Used in much the same way as exclamations like 'oh my goodness' or 'wow'!
Wah piang	Another polite version of 'wah lan'.
Xiong di	Younger brother (Mandarin). Term also used for groomsmen.
Yam Seng	Drink to victory (literal, Cantonese apparently) A must-have toast to congratulate the bride and groom at any Chinese wedding. The longer you draw out the 'Yam' the more blessings will come to the couple. May also be spelled as 'Yum Seng'.
Zap	Slang for 'photocopy'.

Acknowledgements

My thanks to everyone who helped build this book, especially:

- Philip Tatham and his team at Monsoon Books for all the work they put into bringing this book into reality.
- My readers, Alan Pearson, Peter Kraemer, Tan Joo Lee and June Loh, for their feedback and support. Special thanks to Alan who read the first and roughest draft and still encouraged me to persevere.
- Everyone who helped me to fill in the gaps, especially Norshazrin Ismail, Yoon Eng Tong, Ng Yuet Sum and Eliot Lee.
- Lastly and most importantly, my family who has to deal with me on a daily basis.

References

I couldn't have done this without all the materials available on the internet. My particular thanks to the following sites for providing many of the historical details.

www.roots.sg

www.eresources.nlb.gov.sg

www.channelnewsasia.com

www.straitstimes.com

www.mothership.sg

www.asiaone.com

remembersingapore.org

rememberinghdbestates.blogspot.com

lostnfiledsg.wordpress.com

https://www.singstat.cov.sg

For definitions of terms in the various languages found in Singapore, I relied heavily on the following resources:
The Coxford Singlish Dictionary, TalkingCock.com, Colin Goh, Angsana Books.

http://www.singlish.net/category/dictionary/

https://en.wikipedia.org/wiki/Singlish_vocabulary

https://guidesify.com/singlish-phrases-define-singapore/

https://discoversg.com/2018/07/09/hokkien-words-and-phrases/

http://gateways.sg/~TeochewEnglish/WordsPhrases/
TeochewWordsPhrases.asp

Any mistakes in the text are mine and mine alone.